Praise for *The L*

"I can highly recommend this beautifully moving story. Enjoy!"

— Tj, *Reviews by Jessewave*

"*The Boy Next Door* is an engaging tale of a man caught between family and love.

— *Joyfully Reviewed*

"*The Boy Next Door* is a sweet romance with the familiar and well loved theme of friends turned lovers."

— *Long and Short Reviews*

"The love between Jason and Lowell was beautiful and as difficulties between them unfolded the reader was drawn into their lives..."

— Teresa, *Fallen Angel Reviews*

In Hot Pursuit

"Kate McMurray has penned an intriguing tale of love, loss, and adventure within the pages of *In Hot Pursuit*. The addition of subtle details added to the depth of the characters, making this an all-round, enjoyable read."

— *Rainbow Reviews*

LooseId®

ISBN 13: 978-1-61118-374-0
THE BOY NEXT DOOR
Copyright © December 2011 by Kate McMurray
Originally released in e-book format in January 2011

Cover Art by Valerie Tibbs
Cover Layout and Design by April Martinez

DISCLAIMER: Many of the acts described in our BDSM/fetish titles can be dangerous. Please do not try any new sexual practice, whether it be fire, rope, or whip play, without the guidance of an experienced practitioner. Neither Loose Id nor its authors will be responsible for any loss, harm, injury or death resulting from use of the information contained in any of its titles.

This book is an original publication of Loose Id. Each individual story herein was previously published in e-book format only by Loose Id and is a work of fiction. Any similarity to actual persons, events or existing locations is entirely coincidental.

Printed in the U.S.A. by
Lightning Source, Inc.
1246 Heil Quaker Blvd
La Vergne TN 37086
www.lightningsource.com

THE BOY NEXT DOOR

Kate McMurray

Chapter One

Lowell stood on the front lawn of the house he'd just purchased, feeling a sense of dread. He wanted his cramped studio apartment back. He had no business owning a house in the suburbs, let alone a two-story two-bedroom with vinyl siding and a little white fence around the yard. Park a tricycle on the front lawn, and he was confronting his worst fears.

His friend and Realtor, Joanie, strolled out of the house then, all grins. At Lowell's insistence, she had taken him on a brief tour of the house again after the closing that afternoon. He wished he could share in her enthusiasm, but he'd just parted with a lot of money to own this little corner of the suburban nightmare.

He looked at the houses on either side of his. The one to the left was basically identical to his house but had yellow vinyl siding instead of the vaguely bluish white of Lowell's house. There *was* a bike sitting on the lawn of that house, a small one with a pink frame and tassels on the handles. The house to the right had pinkish siding and was immaculately maintained. It looked like a house straight out of Stepford, with a neatly manicured lawn, and a shiny sedan parked in the driveway.

There was something eerily familiar about the whole block too, which Lowell found puzzling since so much of this town looked the same. Each block was basically identical, cookie-cutter houses with lawns and kids and minivans. It also all looked the same as it had when he'd left sixteen years before.

"You know anything about my neighbors?" Lowell asked Joanie when she reached him.

"Sure," she said. She pointed to the house on the right. "That's the Emerson house. They've only been in town for a few years. I don't know them well at all, but rumor has it Tad Emerson is trying to get his house in one of those home and garden magazines." She turned and pointed to the house on the right. "That's the Midland house. Jason Midland's parents owned it, but they died a few years ago, and Jase lives there now."

"Oh. That's terrible about his parents." Jesus God, of course he would move in next to Jason fucking Midland. He looked at Joanie to see if she remembered Jase had been the object of many of Lowell's high school fantasies, but she seemed oblivious. "I didn't realize Jase stayed in town," he said, sounding impressively calm in his own estimation.

"Oh yeah," Joanie said. "I mean, he was living a few towns over for a while after college, but his parents left him the house in their will, and he moved back here after he got divorced."

"Wow, shit, he's divorced?" Lowell wasn't sure why that struck him as more surreal than the elder Midlands' deaths. Part of the reason, he figured, was that he hadn't seen Jase since they were teenagers; it was hard to think of him as an adult. Lowell looked at Joanie. "You still in touch?"

"Eh. Not that so much as I've got my finger on the pulse of Greenbriar gossip." She held out her finger to demonstrate. Then she laughed. "Jeez, Lowell, I missed you. Please don't abandon us again. I'll make selling your house very difficult if I have to do it to keep you here."

Lowell smiled. "I told you, I'm taking care of my mom. I'll be here a while." He took a deep breath. "I think I played on this street as a kid."

"Yeah, Lester Davies used to live on the other end of the block."

"Of course." Lowell wasn't sure that Joanie knew, but he and Jase Midland had been friends as kids. They'd been in the same classes at Fernbrook Elementary, and everything was great until the kids started separating themselves into cliques. Jase had been King of the Jocks, Lowell had little athletic ability, and they'd grown apart. Lowell had been so antagonized by some of the high school jocks that he'd just mourned the friendship and moved on.

Still, he stood there now, as an adult, and had flashes of birthday parties, of Mrs. Midland carrying plates full of cookies into the living room, of building great battle scenes with action figures and Legos up in Jase's room, represented by the street-facing window on the right side of the house. He was hit with a wave of sadness that he didn't want Joanie to witness. He coughed.

"You want to get a drink or something?" he asked. "Celebrate the purchase of my new house?"

"Yes, let's. But we should drive over to Danbury. I like the bars better there."

"Drive." Lowell laughed. "I'm going to have to get a car, aren't I?"

Joanie patted Lowell on the back. "Welcome home, city boy."

* * *

Jase walked into Schuster's and sat at the bar. He'd had an especially aggravating day at work, and then he'd had an especially aggravating fight with his ex-wife Karen, who'd asked him for money again. There were only two things he could think of that would help him calm down. He needed to get drunk, and he needed to get laid. The drunk was something that could be acquired locally, at least, so he sat at the bar in Schuster's and tapped his fingers impatiently.

"Jesus, Jase, calm down," said Neal from behind the bar. He pulled a beer and set it in front of Jase.

"Sorry, I had a shitty day." He took a grateful gulp of the beer. "Can you get some of your flunkies to take over for you tonight? I just dropped Layla off at Karen's parents' house for the weekend, so I'm home free. I was thinking we could take a train down to the city. You can be my wingman."

Neal raised an eyebrow. "Unfortunately, most of my 'flunkies' caught that summer flu thing that's been going around. It's just me behind the bar and Angela waiting tables tonight. If I'm lucky, the new guy is coming in at nine, and if that happens, I'm going over to Russ's because he promised he'd take a look at my car. The engine is making that whirring sound again."

"So you'd rather spend your night with Russ and your car than with me and the city. A city, by the way, that is full of opportunities for sex."

Neal took a moment to think about that. "Well…yeah. As fun as being your wingman is, that rarely pans out in my favor. At least if I stay in town, odds are good my car will get fixed. Then I can drive you to the city myself during your next free weekend. I view that as a net gain."

Jase rolled his eyes. He took another gulp of beer.

"So I heard some interesting news earlier today," Neal said, wiping at a stain on the bar with a rag.

"Yeah?"

"You remember Lowell Fisher?"

Jase blinked. "Sure," he said, hoping it sounded sufficiently casual. He remembered Lowell, all right. They'd been inseparable as boys, but they'd started to drift apart when Jase got serious about baseball, and things between them had gotten a little weird. Then Lowell had to go and become the first openly gay student that Greenbriar High had ever known. So, yeah, he remembered Lowell Fisher.

Neal gave Jase a long look. "He bought the house next door to yours."

Jase felt the surprise like a punch in the face. "He did not."

"Joanie Reickert did the deal. The closing was supposed to go down this afternoon."

Jase couldn't figure out how to respond. "That's interesting."

Neal snorted. "Interesting. Gee. It's like a fucking reunion up in here."

"Speaking of which, Lowell didn't come to ours, did he? I thought no one had seen or heard from him since graduation. Why the hell is he moving back?"

If Neal heard the tinge of resentment in Jase's voice, he didn't let on. "His father died a couple of months ago."

Neal paused, and Jase frowned. He remembered hearing about that. Neal would, of course, know the bigger story. Jase supposed owning a bar meant you heard everything.

Neal went on, "You remember Old Man Fisher died a couple of months ago?"

"Yeah. Liver disease, right?"

"Yep. Apparently his widow isn't coping very well, so Lowell moved back to Greenbriar to take care of her."

"Why not move back into his parents' house?"

Neal squinted at him. "Weren't you and Lowell friends as kids? Surely you can guess."

Jase had heard the rumors. That Old Man Fisher was an alcoholic, that he routinely beat the crap out of both his wife and his son, that Lowell and his father had stopped speaking entirely when Lowell came out. Jase didn't know how much of it was true. If Lowell was getting beaten up routinely, Jase never saw signs of it when they were kids. Which didn't mean anything, of course. Lowell could have been good at hiding it. Jase had been an oblivious kid.

"Bad memories in the house, maybe," Jase said.

"Yeah. Well. Either way, I think business here declined ten percent when Fisher died."

Jase waited for Neal to laugh, but when he looked up, Neal had a serious expression on his face instead. Jase nodded.

"You want another?" Neal gestured toward his now-empty glass.

"Nah. I might go to the city anyway. Good luck with the car."

"Good luck finding a woman willing to take your sorry ass home for the night."

Jase frowned at Neal. He knew Neal was kidding, but he said, "I just don't want to spend my Friday night alone on my couch."

"So hang out with me here. Come with me to Russ's after."

Jase shook his head. "I don't know when we became such old men that we worry more about making sure our cars run than going out."

"Around the same time you had a kid."

"Ha." Jase dropped a five on the bar and left.

He drove home and made sure to glance at the for-sale sign in the yard next to his house. It did indeed have a SOLD! sticker on it now that partially obscured a photo of Joanie Reickert's smiling face. He sat in his car for a long time, just looking at the sign, trying to imagine living next door to Lowell Fisher. He wasn't even sure what Lowell would look like now—if he'd still be as blond as he had been in high school, if he'd still be as skinny, if he'd still smile the same way.

Of all things, Jase did not need Lowell Fisher in his life again.

He made himself get out of the car. On the way to the house, he picked up Layla's bike and wheeled it inside, not wanting it to rust should it rain. He left it on the tiled area just inside the front door. Then he climbed the stairs up to his room, where he gratefully shed his work clothes. He flipped through things in his closet. He'd definitely go out because, yeah, he wanted to get laid, but more, he couldn't stand how quiet the house was when Layla wasn't in it.

He put on a dark T-shirt and a pair of well-fitting jeans, ran a comb through his hair, and stood in front of the mirror, wondering how inconspicuous he looked. Probably it was better if Neal didn't come with him, not for what he was planning now.

He opted to drive instead of taking the train, so he got back in his car and got on I-84 going east. The drive into Manhattan took an hour and a half, and traffic was surprisingly light for a Friday night. He also, miraculously, found parking near the East Village bars he tended to frequent. After he parked, he walked a couple of blocks and ducked into one of his favorite pubs. He strolled up to the bar and ordered a scotch and soda, then turned around to watch what was going on around him.

There was a smorgasbord of beautiful people, mostly men, and Jase leaned back on the bar to observe them. He was content to do that until a blond man caught his eye.

Too young to be Lowell Fisher, but it was a close resemblance to the boy Jase remembered. The guy in the bar was tall and thin, his hair artfully disheveled, his pants tight.

He raised an eyebrow and gestured toward the back of the bar, so Jase followed.

He walked with the blond guy into a back room. Blond Guy turned around and smiled at him, then hooked a finger into Jase's belt loop and pulled him close. Jase smiled. Blond Guy leaned in like he was going to kiss Jase, and Jase put a hand between them. "I don't kiss," he said.

Blond Guy shrugged. He moved his hand until he was undoing the button on Jase's jeans, so Jase reached for Blond Guy's tight pants and echoed his movements, sliding down the zipper when the guy slid down Jase's. Reaching into the guy's pants was almost a relief; getting close enough to smell the other man had Jase hard and wanting.

"What *do* you do?" Blond Guy asked, his hand on Jase's cock.

"Everything else."

Chapter Two

The movers had already taken longer than the estimate had said they would, and they still had to load all of Lowell's belongings into the new house. Lowell marveled at the sheer number of boxes as he watched the movers carry them out of the truck. He was moving from a cramped studio into this big house, but he supposed that he had collected a fair amount of stuff in the sixteen years he'd lived in Manhattan. All those years away in the city, and now he'd moved back to Connecticut, but it hardly felt like a homecoming.

He glanced at his neighbor's house, which was quiet, like no one was home. He wondered if he should go over and say hi once he was settled. Or if Jase would reach out to him.

But he also had to keep an eye on the movers, who were dawdling.

Joanie drove up while the movers were getting the last of Lowell's furniture situated. Lowell beckoned her into the house, and together they looked at the sparsely furnished living room.

"Wow," said Joanie. It wasn't a good "wow."

Lowell frowned. "I guess this is what happens when you move from a tiny apartment to a big house. For what it's worth, the studio felt really crowded."

"On the bright side, you could probably set up your living room as a bowling alley for extra cash."

"Ha ha."

The movers finally wrapped up, and Lowell paid them, making sure to gripe about how long it took and feeling cheated because he was paying by the hour.

When they were gone, Joanie said, "I came by because I figured you'd need a lift to the grocery store for supplies."

"Yeah, thanks, that would be awesome. Do I really have to buy a car?"

"How else do you propose to get around?"

"Cabs? And there are city buses around here, aren't there?"

Joanie laughed. "Oh sweetie. First of all, the only people who take the bus are the poor and the drunk. Second, the closest bus stop is over by the gas station on Park Street, which is more than a mile from here."

"Oh."

"If you want, I can take you to Russ Rogers's garage tomorrow. I know he's trying to sell a couple of old cars he fixed up. Probably he'd cut you a deal since you're a Greenbriar native and all."

"I'll think about it. If I can even drive anymore. It's probably been five years since I've gotten behind the wheel."

"It's like riding a bike."

Lowell doubted that. "I guess this is why I bothered to keep my license up-to-date."

"Come on. Groceries await."

* * *

When they got back to the house, Lowell saw a car in his neighbor's driveway, a little silver compact something or other. He tried not to acknowledge that his neighbor was home, and Joanie didn't seem to notice either. She helped him carry the bags back into his house. *His* house, Lowell kept reminding himself, though it felt like a stranger's still. He relented and told Joanie she could drive him to see Russ the next day, and then he walked her to her car.

Lowell stood on the sidewalk out front and watched Joanie's car disappear down the street. When he turned to walk back to the house, he noticed a little girl standing in his yard. She looked maybe six or seven years old.

"Hi," Lowell said.

"Hi," said the girl. "Are you my new neighbor?"

"Which house do you live in?"

Lowell expected her to point to the Emerson's Practically Perfect Palace. Instead, she pointed to the yellow Midland residence. He took a closer look at the girl. He thought maybe he recognized Jase's eyes on the girl, and maybe there was something familiar about her face, though she had a riot of blonde curls on top of her head instead of Jase's much darker hair. "I live there," she said.

"Then, yes, I'm your new neighbor. Can you tell me your name?" When she hesitated, he said, "My name is Lowell Fisher."

"I'm Layla Midland."

"That's a very pretty name." Very likely Jase's daughter, then. And wasn't that a kick in the teeth? "Is your father at home?"

"Yes. We're going to go bike riding, so I came outside. That's mine." She pointed to the bike he'd seen when he'd closed on the house. It was propped up in the driveway.

Jase himself came out of the garage then, wheeling an adult-sized bike. He looked around for Layla and saw her. He looked surprised, but Lowell could tell by the expression on his face that he recognized who his daughter was talking to.

Jase didn't look that different than he had in high school. Older, sure, and a bit more substantial. He'd filled out, maybe even grown an inch or two, but he still had a baseball player's physique, strong and athletic without being too muscled. He had on jeans and a yellow polo shirt, and his hair had been cut into what Lowell could only think of as a Dad Cut, longish on top, parted to the left. He looked, in other words, like Jase in a Suburban Dad costume. And he was still, in Lowell's estimation, smoking hot. Lowell felt a little embarrassed just looking at him, like it might be obvious from his face that Jase had starred in some of Lowell's better fantasies.

Jase walked up to them. He and Lowell just looked at each other for a long time. He looked so very familiar, and yet there was something missing there. A light in Jase's eyes that had gone dim. Lowell worried about that, wondered what Jase could have gone through in the years since they last saw each other. He extended a hand.

"Hi, Jase," he said. "It's been a while."

"Yeah. Lowell. Hi." His handshake was warm and powerful. Then their hands parted as if nothing had happened.

Layla looked between the two men. "Did you meet already?"

Jase looked down at the girl. Seeing them next to each other made the similarities between them even more noticeable. "Mr. Fisher and I went to school together." He looked up at Lowell. "This is my daughter, Layla."

"Yes, we've met," said Lowell.

"Wow, you really went to school together? And now he's our neighbor?"

"Yes, it looks that way."

"I found out that you lived here after I closed on the house," Lowell said. "Of course, I should have recognized the block. I don't know why I didn't."

"It's been more than twenty years since you've been to my house," Jase said.

"Yeah. Jesus."

Jase wore an intense expression, his eyebrows drawn close together. "Um. So. Maybe we should have dinner together sometime? We could, I don't know, catch up or whatever."

Right, thought Lowell. "Yes, that would be great. Will you be around tomorrow?"

"Yeah, tomorrow. I could do tomorrow. If the weather's nice, you should come over. I could fire up the grill."

"A cookout, Daddy?" Layla asked. "Can we have a cookout?"

"Sure, sweetheart." He ruffled her hair and smiled, some light coming into his eyes. "How does that seem to you, Lowell? Any dietary restrictions I should know about?"

"I stay away from red meat, but anything else is fair game."

"Turkey burgers it is," Jase said.

He smiled again. Oh Lord, Lowell had forgotten how charming that smile was, how perfect Jase's teeth were. It was going to be interesting times, living next to this man.

"Great, tomorrow night, then. Say around seven?"

"Sure."

"Okay, well. I should go in and finish unpacking. Have a good time on your bike ride."

"Thanks," said Jase.

"Bye, Mr. Fisher!" Layla said with a big wave.

Lowell went back into the house. Before he closed the door, he heard Jase admonishing Layla to remember to wear her helmet.

* * *

Jase's head spun as he watched Layla bound back into the house. He'd spent the entire bike ride feeling dizzy and not quite in control. Seeing Lowell again had been more of a shock than he had expected.

He sent Layla upstairs to get washed up for dinner. Then he sat on the couch and proceeded to freak out. Lowell had looked good. He had obviously grown and matured since high school. He was still tall and thin, as he'd been then, but he was no longer skinny. His hair was a few shades darker, less the light blond it had been when they were kids and now more the color of wet sand. It had been unsettling to see him again, to see everything in him that he'd been all those years ago, to instantly recognize him.

His attraction to Lowell had hit him like a punch in the gut too. He'd watched from afar in high school, attributing his interest to the fact that Lowell had come out as gay and was therefore different. He knew better now and was surprised to find himself drawn so strongly. This man, his neighbor, had once been the kid he'd played and run and caught frogs with.

Jase couldn't help but wonder what it would be like to talk to him now, if they'd be friends again, if there was even a possibility of more. This thought was interrupted by the phone ringing. He picked it up and got a stark reminder of why he had to let this daydream go.

"How are you, Jason?" Karen said.

"I'm all right. What do you want?"

She clucked her tongue. "So direct. Well, since you're asking, I thought I'd let you know I'm in the area, staying at my parents' place for a couple of days. I was thinking I could do something with Layla, maybe take her to the city. To a museum or the Bronx Zoo or something. She'd like that, right?"

"Yeah, that would be nice."

"You should come with us."

A warning bell clanged in his head. "I don't think that's a good idea."

She sighed, and it made a hissing noise through the earpiece on the phone. "Look, I just thought... I mean, it would be fun. We'd be a family even if just for the day. You said yourself that it was important to show her that we both still love her."

"And I stand by that. I do show her that, every day. It's you who doesn't show up for her games or school events. When was the last time you saw her play T-ball? Did you even know she's going to a T-ball camp this summer?"

"I—"

"It's fine with me if you take her to the city for the day. I think she would really like that. I'm not going to go with you because it would be a lie. We're not this perfect family anymore. And if you do want to go, only offer if you really plan to do it. I don't want to get her hopes up again." Jase sat on the couch and rubbed his forehead. "Where have you been the last few weeks, anyway?"

"Around," Karen said. "I went to Boston to try to find a job, stayed with some friends there. You remember Ben and Julie?"

"Yeah, I remember. Did you find any work?"

"Not yet, but I got some interviews."

"I thought you were going to try to get something closer to Greenbriar, to spend more time with Layla."

Karen hiss-sighed again. "Come on, Jason. You know there aren't any jobs in western Connecticut. I've exhausted all the possibilities there. At least in a city there are more options."

"So get a job in New York. The commute from here is not so bad."

The argument fell on deaf ears. Jase knew Karen hated Connecticut. He didn't blame her some days—it was bland and suburban—but it was home. Aside from his brief stint in college in Massachusetts, Jase couldn't imagine living anywhere else.

"Well, anyway. I was thinking mine and Layla's big day could be next Saturday. Does that work for you?"

"Yeah, that would be okay."

"And maybe we go back to my parents' house afterward, spend the night there. Give you a night off to do...whatever it is you do when you're alone." She coughed. Jase suspected she didn't want to think very hard about what Jase did when he was left to his own devices.

"That sounds nice."

They got off the phone, and Jase rubbed his face. He wondered if it was foolish to think Karen would follow through with this promise. He suspected that she wasn't so much spending less time with Layla as avoiding Jase altogether. If that was how she wanted to play it, that was fine by him. He'd just as soon keep Layla with him all the time.

Still, he worried that Layla was getting caught in the crossfire between him and Karen, and he hated how upset she got when Karen disappeared. And, in the end, wasn't it his fault Karen vanished the way she did? At Jase's urging, she'd quit her job when she'd found out she was pregnant with Layla, and had never quite gotten back on her feet again. More to the point, he was the one who had hurt her.

He was the one who had created this whole messy situation. She'd been the one to file for divorce, but he knew the failure of their marriage was largely his fault.

He stared at the phone for a long moment and wanted to scream. The reason he'd destroyed the lives of his wife and his daughter was tangled up in his attraction to his neighbor in a way that made him uneasy. And still, he couldn't help but think about Lowell. He got up and walked over to the bookcase. There were a bunch of old photo albums on a shelf there. Jase paged through a few of the albums before finding the one he wanted, which was mostly pictures of him when he was Layla's age. Layla came into the living room and sat next to him on the couch as he flipped through it.

"Why are you looking at old pictures?" she asked.

"I was looking for something in particular," said Jase, still flipping. Finally, he found it. His seventh birthday party. He pointed to the picture. It showed Jase with his arm thrown around another boy, both of them looking like they were on the verge of wrestling each other, but they had big grins on their faces. "That's me. And that's Mr. Fisher from next door."

"What?" Layla laughed like she didn't believe it.

"We were very good friends when we were your age. We were in the same class in first grade."

"Like me and Susie?"

"Yeah, a lot like you and Susie." Only not at all, because then he and Lowell had hit puberty, and everything changed.

Chapter Three

When Joanie pulled into Russ Rogers's auto shop, Lowell was hit with a shot of déjà vu. He could remember coming to this very auto shop with his father when he was a kid. The elder Rogers had presided over car inspections and major repairs for almost everyone in town.

"Technically Russ's dad owns it," Joanie explained as she parked. "But he's mostly retired, so Russ runs the show. You should take his word for it that whatever he's trying to sell you is a good car. Russ is a wizard with cars. He can fix anything. In my head, I sort of picture him like the Fonz. He just has to put his hand on the hood and go, 'Heeey,' and it works."

Lowell laughed. The Russ Rogers he remembered was a scrawny, nerdy kid with reddish hair and freckles. He thought he'd remembered hearing that Russ gone off to Rensselaer to study engineering and so was surprised to hear he was working as a mechanic these days.

"He studied mechanical engineering," Joanie said when Lowell asked. "He finished his degree and moved back to Greenbriar. Roomed with Neal Schusterman for a while, actually. You remember Neal?"

"I remember Neal," Lowell said. Mostly what he remembered about Neal was stealing kisses backstage during their class's production of *The Music Man*, in which Lowell starred as Harold, and Neal worked crew. Lowell found it hard to resent Neal in retrospect, since the poor guy had been still finding his way, but at the time, Lowell had felt used, like he was just a convenient cypher for Neal's curiosity or experimentation or whatever it was. Not that he hadn't enjoyed the kissing. Neal had been a cute boy, after all. Lowell wondered if he'd ever come out, but couldn't bring himself to ask Joanie.

Russ came strolling out of the auto shop as Joanie pulled into the parking lot. He was still a little scrawny, still had the reddish hair and the freckles, but he looked older, for sure. Like life had beat him up a little. Although, on further reflection, Lowell wondered if everyone just looked so much older because it had been so long since he'd seen anyone from his graduating class besides Joanie.

Still, Russ smiled as Joanie and Lowell got out of the car, the skin around his eyes crinkling as he wiped grease off his hands with a rag. He tossed the rag aside and gave Joanie a quick hug. Then he held out his hand to Lowell. "Nice to see you again," he said cordially.

"Yeah. Thanks for seeing me on a Sunday."

"It's no problem. Joanie says you're looking for a car."

"Yeah, I suppose I am. I haven't actually ever owned one, so this is a big deal." He raised an eyebrow in a way that he hoped showed he was kidding.

Russ laughed. "You're, what, thirty-four? And you've never owned a car?"

"I've been living in the city."

"Come with me." Russ led them around to the back of the shop. There were three cars parked there: a red Trans Am, a navy blue Ford Taurus, and a green Volkswagen Jetta that looked a few generations old. "Here's what I got for sale."

"I've always kind of wanted a Jetta," Lowell said. "I figured if I ever had to own a car, I'd want a cute little one. That one looks like it's seen better days, though."

"It just needs a new coat of paint. The engine runs great, and the structure is sound. You want to give it a test drive?"

"I can't guarantee I won't crash it," Lowell said.

Russ laughed, but then realized Lowell was serious. "Oh."

"Lowell hasn't driven a car in a while," Joanie said.

Russ told them to wait for a moment. He ran inside and came back out a few minutes later with a ring full of keys. "This is the key for the Jetta," he said, holding it up. He handed it to Lowell. "Maybe stay off the highway, but drive it around a little to see how you like it."

"Okay," said Lowell, getting into the car. He hadn't driven a car in so long that it felt like he was on the wrong side of the vehicle. Joanie got in the passenger side and made a point of buckling the seat belt. Lowell adjusted the seat and the mirrors and then he put the key in the ignition and turned it. The car hummed to life. "So far so good."

"Let's see what you remember how to do," said Joanie.

"You're putting your life in my hands." Lowell put the car in reverse and craned his neck around to make sure he wasn't going to hit anything. After a tentative start, he got the car moving out of the parking lot and onto Brookfield Road. He took it up to forty miles per hour and was amazed that he had the memory in his muscles to pilot the thing.

"This thing handles smoothly," Lowell said as he turned down a side street.

"It's that Fonzie thing. Russ just knows how to make cars run like this."

"I'm thinking that's not a Volkswagen engine under the hood."

"Like you would know."

They drove around for fifteen minutes before pulling back into the auto shop's parking lot.

Russ walked over to them. "I see you didn't crash it."

Lowell climbed out of the car. "It would get me around town," he said as he closed the door. "How much do you want for it?"

Russ named a figure that was lower than Lowell was expecting. "Is there something seriously wrong with it that I don't know about?"

"No, no, it's in fine working order. This is just not that valuable a car."

"Oh."

"I mostly fix old cars as a hobby. I'm not really looking to turn a profit. That particular car belonged to a teenager who bought it from God knows where, and it had basically stopped running by the time he left for college, so his parents were going to scrap it. I begged and pleaded a little, and they let me have it gratis. I'm basically just charging you for the parts and labor it took to fix it. See, I replaced the engine, then..." Russ launched into a long explanation of all the repairs he'd done, most of which didn't make sense to Lowell, but his conclusion was satisfactory: Russ knew his shit. He wouldn't sell Lowell a lemon.

They went into the auto shop, and Lowell wrote Russ a check and thanked him.

"You want a new paint job, let me know. I can get that done in a weekend."

"Thanks. I'd leave it with you now, but I have kind of a transportation emergency. I can't make Joanie chauffeur me around all the time. But I might take you up on the new paint job in a few weeks."

"Not a problem," said Russ.

* * *

Jase was surprised to find himself standing in the middle of his bedroom, agonizing over what to wear. "This is not a date," he reminded himself out loud. "Fuck it." He pulled on a clean shirt before running downstairs.

Layla was sitting on the couch in the living room. She'd set up a motley crew of plastic toys, Legos, and Barbies on the coffee table. They seemed to be arranged in a baseball configuration, with squares of construction paper used as bases.

"Looks good," Jase said.

"Barbie is on the Yankees," Layla said. When Jase sat down on the couch, he saw that Layla had drawn a crude approximation of the Yankee's logo on Barbie's white T-shirt.

"Cool," Jase said. "Are the Yankees winning?"

Layla nodded. "They're playing the Sox."

The Sox team seemed to be composed mostly of comic book action figures. Karen had argued with Jase about how he indulged Layla's more boyish interests, but Jase didn't see the harm in letting her play with stereotypical boys' toys, and besides, she'd been so happy when he'd unearthed the box of his old comic books from the attic. He liked that they had common interests, things to bond over. She liked Barbies and coloring books as much as she liked baseball and action figures, so let her have the toys, he'd figured.

He ran a hand over Layla's blonde head and wondered if he spoiled her too much. He'd felt so petty when he and Karen had separated, and he'd been determined not only to be the better parent but to be the one Layla liked better. He knew that was foolish, that it was selfish and a little spiteful, but he also couldn't bear the thought of Layla choosing Karen over him, of her ever moving out of his house.

"I hate to end the game," he said, "but I think you might have to call a rain delay so you can come help me make dinner."

She looked for a moment like she was going to complain, but then she shrugged. "Okay. Can I color while you cook?"

"Sure." Which, of course, meant dragging out coloring books and crayons and more clutter, but she'd been charming and well-behaved all day, and he found it hard to say no to her on days like that. In an effort to not be too indulgent, he said, "You can color if you clean up some of your baseball game first."

Layla nodded and dragged the plastic bin where most of her dolls lived over to the coffee table. She started to put things away, then said, "I want to leave the bases on the table so I remember where Barbie was. She made it to third base with two outs, bottom of the seventh."

Jase chuckled and agreed to leave the bases and Barbie on the table, but everything else went into the box. She put the rest of her toys away while Jase fired up the grill. He was in the kitchen, in the process of smashing ground turkey into patties, when Layla came down the stairs with a stack of coloring books and her box of crayons. "Can I sit at the picnic table while you cook?"

"Yes, but stay away from the grill."

"Okay, Daddy." She grinned and went outside.

* * *

Lowell tried to play it cool, tried not to show how taken aback he'd been when Jase opened the door. Jase stood there in a loose blue Oxford shirt, untucked, with the top couple of buttons undone and the sleeves rolled up to his elbows. He had it on over long khaki shorts and an expensive-looking pair of sandals. Who knew preppy could look so enticing?

Jase motioned him inside. He took a gander at the house and was surprised at how familiar everything looked. Lowell figured some furniture had moved, and certainly the art on the walls was more Jase's taste than his parents', but it did seem largely the same as it had when they were kids.

"Layla's out back watching the grill for me. We should get back there before she lights the yard on fire," Jase said. Lowell followed him through the house.

Layla sat at a picnic table with a coloring book and a box of crayons. Jase watched her for a moment before walking over to the grill. "Have a seat, Lowell," Jase said.

So Lowell sat across from Layla. "Hi," he said. "How are you today?"

"Good. Daddy said we're going to have turkey burgers and potato salad."

"Great! Those are some of my favorites."

Layla concentrated on her coloring for a minute, then looked up. "Daddy said you went to school together when you were little boys."

"We did, yes."

"I have a friend at school named Susie."

"That's good. What grade are you in?"

"I just finished first grade. I start second grade next."

Lowell wasn't entirely sure how to interact with a girl this young. Jase went about grilling burgers and occasionally looked over his shoulder to see how they were doing, but generally stayed out of the conversation.

"Mr. Fisher?" Layla asked at one point. "Do you work in an office like Daddy?"

Lowell wasn't quite sure what to do with the question, especially when he realized he had no idea what Jase did for a living. "I don't work in an office," he said. "And you can call me Lowell."

Layla looked down at her coloring and very carefully colored a bear brown. "Daddy says it's more respectful to call people by their last names."

"That's true, but once you get to know someone, you can call them whatever they like to be called. I'm your neighbor, and I'd like to be your friend, so you can call me Lowell."

"Okay, Lowell." She looked up and smiled. It was a great, toothy smile. Jase's smile. Lowell had a hard time reconciling this girl with the kid he'd known as a boy.

Jase brought over a plate full of burgers and placed it on the table. "I left some things inside. Give me two minutes." He disappeared into the house and came back with a plastic container full of potato salad and a baggie full of plastic utensils. Then he grabbed ketchup and barbecue sauce from over by the grill and put those on the table too. He ran back inside and came back with a stack of paper plates and a six-pack of soda and put those on the table. "Dig in," he said.

Once everyone started eating, Jase asked, "So what are you up to these days?"

"I'm working as a graphic designer," said Lowell. "Mostly websites. I had a day job at an advertising company until recently, but I decided to go freelance full time when I moved up here. What do you do?"

"You're looking at middle management," he said. "I'm a supervisor in the sales department over at Slater-Grosse Pharmaceuticals."

"Oh." He thought that sounded like a perfectly dreadful way to spend one's days. Judging from the look on Jase's face, he thought so too.

The rest of the dinner conversation passed politely, with Layla occasionally interjecting to talk about school or the T-ball camp she was going to that summer. Lowell was somewhat surprised that the only mention of Jase's ex-wife came when Layla asked where Lowell had moved from. Lowell said New York City, and Layla said she was going there the next weekend with her mother. Jase didn't react to the mention of Layla's mother at all, so Lowell just acknowledged that and let it go.

After they finished eating, Layla wandered over to the old swing set in the backyard and got on one of the swings.

"I can't believe that's still here," Lowell said.

"Yeah, my parents never got around to disassembling it. I already had Layla when I moved back in, so it made sense to keep it. I did a little bit of work on it too. I replaced all the chains, oiled some of the joints. It was pretty old and rusty when I moved here."

Lowell wanted to ask more personal questions but didn't want to pry or push Jase out of the good mood he seemed to be in. Instead he said, "Have you been back here long?"

"Just since the divorce. Or, really, since Karen kicked me out. That was about two years ago."

Lowell raised an eyebrow. He was very curious about the end of Jase's marriage. Jase gestured toward Layla. Lowell guessed that meant Jase didn't want to talk about it in front of his daughter. Or at all.

Jase and Lowell cleaned up the plates and condiments while Layla swung, and the sun started to go down. When everything was clean, Jase said, "Okay, kiddo, time for bed."

"But Daddy!"

"We're getting up to go to T-ball camp tomorrow, so you need some sleep."

"I want to play with Lowell! I can show him my dolls and my coloring books and—"

"Some other time. Lowell lives next door. You can see him a lot if you want. But now you have to go to bed."

Layla pouted but dutifully marched into the house.

Jase motioned for Lowell to follow him back inside. "Have a seat on the couch in the living room. I'll put her to bed."

"I can go, if you need me to."

"No, don't. She'll be fine. She's usually out once I turn off the lights. Have a seat. We'll have a beer or something."

"Okay."

Jase climbed the stairs. Lowell could hear Jase and Layla talking but couldn't make out the words. He sat on the couch and looked around the room while he waited, noticed the photos of Layla on the mantel next to the photo of Jase's parents. He sighed, thinking about the lost years between them. Then he noticed the Barbie on the coffee table, sitting on what looked like a baseball diamond made of construction paper. He chuckled, feeling out of his element in a house with a child.

When Jase came back downstairs, Lowell said, "She lives with you?"

"Yeah. Karen—my ex—has been having some problems. She…moves a lot. We decided it was better for Layla to have stability." Jase frowned. Lowell moved over on the couch to make room for him, and Jase sat. "Layla spends one weekend a month with Karen's parents, and Karen visits with her pretty often. It's not like I think Karen is a bad mother or anything. Just…you know."

"You want Layla with you all the time."

Jase shrugged. "Yeah. She's my baby girl. I want to make sure I see her grow up."

"She seems happy."

Jase smiled. "Yeah, thanks. I think she is."

"What about you?"

"What about me?"

"How are you?"

The silence that stretched as Jase contemplated the question was answer enough, but he looked off at something in the distance and said, "Eh." He ran a hand through his hair. "It's been a weird last couple of years." He gestured vaguely toward the wall.

"Have you dated much since your divorce?" He hoped the question sounded casual. What struck Lowell more than anything was that Jase seemed lonely.

"No, I haven't really dated anybody."

"You separated two years ago? That's a long time to go without sex."

Jase smirked, and something of the kid Lowell remembered returned to his face. "I didn't say I hadn't had sex."

"Ah."

Jase turned to face him. "What about you? Have you been seeing anybody?"

"I was kind of seeing this guy right before I moved, but he's even more phobic of the suburbs than I am, so that's over now."

"Guy? So you're still...?"

"Gay? It doesn't go into remission, Jase."

Jase nodded and looked over Lowell carefully. Lowell felt scrutinized in a way that made him uncomfortable. Jase said, "I know, it's just...it's strange picturing someone you haven't seen since you were seventeen as a grown-up with a sex life."

"I suppose."

Jase looked like he wanted to ask another question but thought better of it. Instead he leaned on the couch and let his head rest on the back. He turned to look at Lowell. "I thought this would be weirder, seeing you again, but it's not. It's like meeting a stranger in some ways, but we were friends for a long time too."

"Yeah, but it's a little weird."

"Maybe," Jase said, sitting up again. "It's too bad we drifted apart in high school."

"Well, you know how it is. You were a jock, I was an art fag. It never would have worked out."

Lowell meant it as a joke, but Jase seemed to take it seriously, nodding and looking contemplative. He smiled faintly. "There was something else too, but I don't think I was mature enough to handle it."

"What something else?"

Jase waved his hand. "It's not important. And it doesn't matter anyway. It's in the past."

"Okay."

Jase looked at Lowell then, straight in the eye, and Lowell felt something crackle between them. That surprised him. It couldn't be mutual attraction. Could it? He was definitely attracted to Jase; he'd jerked off as a teenager thinking of the boy, but the man in front of him was so much better, full-grown and solid, handsome and interesting. But he was also straight. He'd been married; he had a kid. There's no way he'd be attracted to Lowell. Right?

Jase looked away, and the spell was broken, which was just as well because Lowell found himself panicking. "I should probably go home," he said.

"You don't have to."

Lowell stood and stretched his arms over his head. "I'm tired. I got up early this morning to buy a Volkswagen from Russ Rogers."

"Yeah, I saw it in the driveway."

"Turns out I need wheels to get around this two-bit town."

Jase laughed. He stood too. "Russ would be the guy to see about that."

"Plus, you know, it's Sunday. You probably have to go to work tomorrow. I wouldn't want to overstay my welcome."

Jase followed Lowell over to the door. "It's kind of nice having a friendly neighbor. The previous owners of that house were an elderly couple who wouldn't talk to me because they couldn't believe I'd sinned by getting divorced."

"Gotta love the Catholic population of Greenbriar."

"Yeah." Jase opened the front door. He looked sad for a moment.

"Well," Lowell said, stepping into the doorway. "A gay man bought their house. That seems like karmic retribution to me."

Jase smiled. "I'll see you around, Lowell."

"Goodnight, Jase."

Chapter Four

Jase reflected on the week that had come and gone, feeling like it had been a week just like every other, only maybe it wasn't, because something felt different. He'd gone to work, yes, and he'd hated himself every moment he sat at his desk, and there were bad meetings and too much to do. Layla had skinned her knee at camp, and then he'd burned dinner on Wednesday but had made Layla's day by giving up and ordering pizza. He'd been kind of surprised when Karen followed through on her promise to take Layla to the city, expecting her to flake like she did so often these days. They were spending the night at Karen's parents, so now he was by himself in his house, feeling drained and lonely.

He looked out the window and saw his neighbor's battered Volkswagen sitting in the driveway. Without giving it much thought, he grabbed his wallet and keys and walked next door.

Lowell answered the door looking disheveled but kind of delicious. He had on a faded T-shirt and running shorts, and his hair was sticking out in several directions. He was sweaty, like he'd been working out, but something about the way Lowell smelled undid Jase. Lowell was sweaty, yes, but the smell was sweet and masculine. Jase wondered what it would be like to be closer to that body, to rub against the stubble on his chin, to take a deeper breath. He wanted to push Lowell against a wall and do unspeakable things to him. He took a step back, already hard, hoping Lowell's gaze would stay above his waist. He forced himself to smile. "Hey," he said.

"Hi." Lowell looked mildly embarrassed. "Sorry I smell like a locker room. I just got back from a run."

"It's okay." Saying he liked how Lowell smelled would probably have taken it too far. "I was wondering if you were doing anything tonight."

"Not as such. Why? Did you have something in mind?"

"I thought we could go out, get a drink or something. Karen took Layla for the weekend, so I'm just rattling around in my house."

"Okay, sure. Um. Give me ten minutes?"

Lowell's house had the same basic layout as Jase's, with the living room to the left of the front door, and a staircase to the right. Lowell indicated the couch in the living room. "Have a seat. Sorry for my house's unfurnished state. Feel free to watch TV or something." Then he ran upstairs.

Jase sat on the couch and heard water running through the pipes, indicating Lowell was in the shower. He looked around the room. It was tasteful. Sparse, yes, but all of Lowell's furniture and decorations had a sleek, modern aesthetic. Jase supposed this would make sense, since Lowell was a graphic designer. He'd probably spent time carefully picking things out instead of filling his house with whatever was easily available.

There were several magazines on the coffee table, most of them art or design related, though there was a men's fashion magazine that had a really hot model on the cover. Jase decided it was safer to avoid that one, so he picked up an art magazine and flipped through it, barely registering what appeared in any of the pictures.

He kept thinking that Lowell lived in a completely different world than he did, one that was urbane and beautiful, not cluttered and full of kids and baseball games. For the first time since they'd been reunited, Jase started to feel a little bit of that breach between them that had formed when they were teenagers.

As promised, Lowell bounded down the stairs ten minutes later, wearing a navy blue T-shirt and a pair of madras shorts, his hair toweled dry. "Let me just figure out where I left my sandals," he said, disappearing into the back of the house. He returned a moment later, sandals on his feet and keys in his hand.

"I'll drive," Jase said.

"Okay." Lowell grinned. The grin was completely disarming, the sort of smile that transformed Lowell from a good-looking guy to a knockout. Jase felt that smile in his gut.

Lowell locked up and followed Jase over to his driveway, and they got in the car. Jase said, "I figured we'd just go to Schuster's. Since Neal Schusterman took over, he's expanded the menu pretty extensively."

"Yeah? Okay, that sounds good." He shook his head. "I remember Schuster's being the place all the grown-ups went. I bet my old man wasted a lot of money in there."

Jase didn't say anything but instead put the car in gear and drove over to the bar. They rode in relative silence, punctuated by Lowell occasionally asking questions about things they drove past. Jase found Lowell's proximity a little disconcerting but took a deep breath and just tried to go with it.

As they walked into Schuster's, they nearly collided with Russ, who was on his way out of the restaurant. He looked surprised to see them. "Uh, hey," he said, running a hand through his hair like he was nervous. "How's the VW working out for you, Lowell?"

"Good so far. It seems to run well. Although you could fit everything I know about cars in the backseat of the Jetta with room to spare."

Russ smiled. "Hey, Jase, how goes it?"

"It goes fine."

"Well, I gotta run." He looked at Jase, then at Lowell, then back at Jase. "See you around."

Jase watched Russ walk out to his car before going into Schuster's. He felt a little confused but shook it off. Once they were inside, Lowell followed him to a table toward the back, next to a large window that overlooked Closter Park.

"Wow, this is nicer than I was expecting," Lowell said.

"Have you ever been here?"

"No, I don't think I have. Not even for dinner."

"Back when we were kids, they pretty much only served hamburgers. You might be happy to know it's got a more sophisticated menu now. Neal's cousin Charlotte is the head chef. She trained at some fancy restaurant in the city."

Neal walked over then and handed them each a menu. Jase had the menu committed to memory, but he took one anyway. He looked up in time to see Neal and Lowell exchange a strange look. "Hello, Neal," Lowell said.

"Good to see you again, Lowell." Neal blinked, then addressed the table at large. "We finally got that summer ale in, so that's on tap now. Special tonight is penne à la vodka. You boys want anything to drink?"

"I'll have the summer ale," said Jase.

Lowell scratched his chin. "You have anything that tastes less beer-y?"

Neal laughed. "I've got a cider on tap."

"That'll work."

Neal left to get their drinks. Jase goggled at Lowell. "Not a fan of beer?"

"No, not really. I'm not much of a drinker. Just never acquired a taste for it, I guess."

"How did you get through college if you don't like beer?"

Lowell raised an eyebrow. "I think you and I had very different college experiences, my friend."

"Oh come on, it couldn't have been that different."

Lowell put his menu down and raised an eyebrow. "I know how your story goes. You got a baseball scholarship to UMass, right? So you went, played baseball, probably studied something liberal artsy. English?"

"Communications."

"Right. I bet you partied a lot, were maybe a member of a fraternity."

"Guilty. Phi Sig."

"Uh-huh. So you drank a lot of beer, slept with a lot of women."

"Well, I drank a lot of beer for sure, but I didn't sleep with that many women. I met my ex-wife in college. We started dating when we were juniors."

"Still. I fled Greenbriar and went straight to New York City. I majored in art at NYU. I had a gay roommate my freshman year, who I did not sleep with, for the record, but with whom I went out a lot. We got fake IDs and snuck into gay clubs where mostly we drank pink cocktails and danced a lot. No fraternities for me. I never would have gotten into one anyway. They tend not to take the gay kids."

"Or they do, if the gay kids stay in the closet."

That was exactly the wrong thing to say, Jase realized. The way Lowell's eyes scanned Jase's face made Jase feel like he was being examined. Lowell said, "Yeah, sure, probably some of that went around. Anyway, I'm sure I was really annoying in college, and I tended to queen it up a bit, wearing my homo status like a badge. It took me a while to get over myself."

"It's not like you kept any of it a secret in high school."

"True. Although at least in college, I got to date men publicly. You'll recall I took Joanie Reickert to prom."

"I do remember that."

"You got to take a real date. Weren't you going out with Shari deRossi back then?"

"Yep." Jase was a little surprised that Lowell remembered.

"So. College for me was like an all-you-can-eat buffet. I was free of my parents, and there were a lot of other gay kids around, so I found my little niche and fucked who I wanted to, and I also fell in love with the city. Things are a little different there than they are in New England."

"That's true," said Jase, who was a little hung up on the image of Lowell—the eighteen-year-old Lowell he remembered—fucking other men. He considered asking what clubs Lowell went to, but he didn't want to know if there'd been some close encounter, if they'd ever been to the same places. He didn't trust his face not to betray him if Lowell were to mention some place he'd gone to also.

Instead, he pretended to look at the menu as he watched Lowell, who ran a hand over his drying hair as he decided what to eat. Lowell still looked a little flushed from the heat that day, and Jase couldn't help but notice how smooth and soft his skin looked, how blue his eyes seemed. He sighed, then immediately regretted it.

Lowell looked up. "What?"

"Nothing. Just deciding what to eat."

Lowell nodded and went back to perusing the menu.

Neal came back a minute later and took their orders. He didn't seem especially talkative tonight. "Everything okay?" Jase asked.

"Yeah, it's fine." Neal looked down. "Russ and I had a completely stupid fight."

"I'm sorry to hear that," Jase said. "What was it about?"

Neal shook his head. "Nothing, just some stupid shit. I kind of picked a fight, and then he got mad and walked out of here."

Jase glanced at Lowell, who seemed to be following the conversation with some interest. Jase raised an eyebrow, which prompted Lowell to say, "It sounds just like high school. It's kind of surreal."

"Maybe not enough has changed since high school," said Neal. "Same old people, same old shit, only now we've got kids and mortgage payments to worry about too." He turned then and walked back to the kitchen.

There was a Yankees game on the TV over the bar, so Jase and Lowell spent the next few minutes talking about baseball. Lowell had only a casual knowledge of the sport, admitting that most of what he knew about the Yankees' lineup was picked up via osmosis while he lived in New York. "Why bother to pay attention when everything you need to know is on the back page of the *Post* someone left on the subway?" he said.

Neal brought out their food and went back to tending the bar. They dug in. At one point, Jase looked up and noticed that Lowell seemed to be on guard. "What's up?" Jase asked.

"I feel like everyone is looking at me." Lowell peered around the room.

Jase looked too. Everyone seemed absorbed in their meals. "You're crazy. Nobody here even knows who you are."

"Maybe. I feel sometimes like I'm a curiosity. I'll see someone around town, and they'll squint at me like they remember me and are waiting for me to do something outlandish. I mean, you're right, it's probably in my head, but still."

Jase watched Lowell eat for a moment, then said the first thing that occurred to him. "Why did you do it?"

Lowell frowned. "Do what?"

"Why'd you come out in high school? Why put yourself through the wringer like that?" He added more quietly, "Didn't you make yourself the curiosity?"

Lowell sighed and put down his fork. "I think mostly I did it to piss off my father."

"I bet you accomplished that."

"Oh yeah. But at least I never had to hide. Once everyone knew, once it was out there, people either accepted or condemned me. It was a good way to know who my real friends were."

Jase took that a little personally. "It's too bad we didn't stay friends in high school."

"Water under the bridge. Besides, you would never have heard the end of it if you'd palled around with me instead of your baseball buddies. Most of the jocks were calling me Lola, remember that?"

"Yeah. Probably I did too."

"Not to my face."

"Not because I wanted to."

"Tony Scarlotti started that trend, I think. I found him really intimidating."

"Yeah, me too. He used to threaten bodily harm if I didn't hit at least one home run every week."

Lowell laughed. "Jesus. Did that help you?" He thought about that for a moment. "Wait, didn't you have the regional home run record senior year?"

Jase nodded. "I guess he helped." He grinned.

Lowell laughed again. "That's crazy. God, I hated Tony Scarlotti."

"If it makes you feel better, he failed a class, lost his baseball scholarship, and had to drop out of college. Last I heard he was working as a blackjack dealer at Mohegan Sun."

"Whoa, really?"

"What goes around, comes around. I heard he was a shitty ballplayer in college anyway. Tore a rotator cuff as a freshman and was never quite the same after that."

"What about you? Why aren't you playing for the Yankees now?"

Jase sighed. He glanced at the TV over the bar. "I don't know if I ever would have been competitive enough to make it to the majors. I did all right in college. I could hit a ball and was a decent first baseman. And I could run fast. I was always a good runner. But—I don't know. I guess I let Karen convince me that there was no real future in baseball, so instead I got the sales job at Slater-Grosse and worked my way up through the ranks."

"But you don't especially like your job."

Jase took a sip of his beer. "It's fine."

"Still, you gave up baseball for the sake of your ex-wife."

"Well, now for the sake of my daughter, but yeah. She was probably right, you know. Making the majors, that was a pipe dream."

Lowell sat back in his chair and looked thoughtful. "You surprise me."

"How so?"

"I don't know. I never expected you to be so modest. And you've made sacrifices for the people you care about. I admire that."

"Oh. Thanks." Jase didn't know how to react, but he did know that part of him very much wanted to be admired, especially by Lowell.

"I guess you have to compromise as an adult. If it were up to me, I'd spend my days in Central Park, painting."

"I kind of wondered if you'd become an actor," said Jase.

"I was not a very good actor. Sure, I could hold my own in a high school production of *The Music Man*, but I took a theater class my freshman year of college and was floored by how much better everyone else was. I was much better suited for the visual arts program. I may not even be a good painter, but I can design things that people like."

"That's something."

"Yeah. You've got talents too. It's a shame for them to be wasted on your job."

Jase shook his head. "What can I do? Throw a baseball? Layla loves it, so we play catch sometimes, but that's the extent of it for me these days. She's been going to a coed T-ball-slash-baseball camp, actually."

"Really? That must be fun for you."

"I worry it's partly me reliving my childhood through her, and I try not to be one of *those* fathers, if you know what I mean."

"You mean you don't punch out the fathers on the opposing team?" Lowell chuckled.

"Nope. But Layla seems to genuinely enjoy the sport."

"So maybe she'll make the Olympic softball team."

"One can hope," Jase said with a smile.

Neal brought them a second round as they were finishing dinner. Lowell abandoned his plate, so Jase did likewise, taking a long sip of the beer.

"Makes me wonder how we were friends as kids," Lowell said. "I was a terrible athlete."

"You could run pretty fast, though. Besides, mostly we, what, ran around our yards, swung on the swing set, played with Transformers. Normal boy things. I didn't really take baseball seriously until high school."

"Which is about when we parted ways," Lowell pointed out.

"Yeah, but baseball wasn't the only reason."

Lowell folded his arms across his chest. "What were the other reasons?" he asked.

Jase frowned. "You were there. I don't know. Things changed. We grew apart."

"We seem to be getting along pretty well now."

"Well, sure. We're grown-up now."

Lowell uncrossed his arms and leaned on the table with his elbows. Jase leaned forward a little too, close enough to smell Lowell's shampoo, which smelled of pine. Quietly, Lowell said, "Part of me always wondered if you were ashamed of me. If you went off with your jock friends and left me in the dust because you didn't want to be associated with me anymore."

God, was that what Lowell really thought? "No, I was never ashamed of you." The emotion Jase felt was closer to "terrified." "I didn't know how to relate to you, I guess, especially after you came out, but I was never ashamed of you. I don't know. I was a stupid teenager."

"That's good to know, I suppose," Lowell said.

Jase nodded. He still felt a little terrified of Lowell. Jase was afraid of what Lowell represented, of what he could be. Jase was enjoying the rekindling of their friendship a great deal, which was also terrifying. He didn't know what he wanted from Lowell, didn't know what he could have, what he could dare to hope for. More to the point, though, he was terrified of what all that meant. Anonymous sex in a bar was one thing, but this palpable yearning for Lowell was something else entirely, something new and scary, something Jase could never allow himself to have.

"Thanks for dinner tonight," he said. "I go a little crazy when Layla's away. It helps to have someone else to talk to."

"I bet. I'm happy to oblige. It's nice to have friends here, I have to say. Joanie and I kept in touch, but otherwise, I just blew everyone off when I graduated, and I wasn't expecting to be welcomed back so warmly."

"People mature, the town changes. You may have been the first openly gay student at Greenbriar High, but you weren't the last."

"Yeah? Well, that's good." Lowell seemed genuinely pleased.

"One might say you're a trailblazer. I admire that about you, that you had the courage to do that."

"I wonder sometimes if it was more stupidity than courage."

"But you said so yourself, you got to be who you are, be with who you wanted. There's a lot to be said for that."

Lowell gave Jase a long, appraising look. "Yeah, there certainly is."

Chapter Five

Lowell looked at his watch as he walked into Schuster's and realized he was early to meet Joanie, so he sat at the bar and prepared to wait. Neal walked over to Lowell and asked what he'd like to drink.

"Just a diet soda."

"Sure," said Neal. He poured the soda while Lowell looked around the bar.

"Nobody's here."

"It is a Tuesday. Not exactly our busiest night of the week."

"Oh."

Neal slid the glass in front of Lowell. "So how are you finding Greenbriar?"

"Okay. Better than I expected."

"Really?"

"Yeah. I have to admit, I was kind of expecting mobs and pitchforks, and I do get some strange looks, but mostly people leave me alone." Lowell took a sip of his soda.

"Maybe people don't remember."

"Sure, maybe. I'm guessing, though, that anyone who was here twenty years ago remembers. On the other hand, Jase tells me there have been other out gay kids at GHS."

"Yeah," Neal said with a nod. "Actually, two girls went to prom together last year."

"Really?" Lowell laughed. "That's wonderful."

Neal smiled. "I thought so too, but it was a huge scandal. A bunch of parents threatened not to send their kids to the prom, and then there was this movement to have two different proms, and it was a mess. Eventually things calmed down, and the prom went on anyway with everyone in attendance, but I think it's too much to hope that the stuffy residents of Greenbriar learned a lesson about how there's nothing threatening about a couple of girls—or boys—who love each other." He leaned against the shelf at the back of the bar.

"It's so weird. I mean, good for those girls. I came out and what did I get for it? Shunned by everyone in town."

"That's a little exaggerated."

"Maybe so. Also, my father punched me in the stomach hard enough to leave a bruise, so there's that." Lowell rubbed the spot. He and Neal hadn't had the opportunity to speak much since he had moved back, and he wondered how much Neal remembered. The strange thing was that they had never been especially close friends, and yet Neal was the one who knew Lowell's secrets, knew his father's secrets. "He never hit me on the face. He thought we deserved to have the crap kicked out of us routinely, especially me, his fairy son. Sometimes he seemed to think that he was beating some masculinity into me. But somewhere in his foggy brain, he knew enough not to want people to know."

"Shit."

"You knew that, though."

"Yeah. I came over to your house to drop off some stuff once, and I showed up in the middle of a fight. Your old man had a belt in his hand. I didn't think he was going to put it on his pants."

Lowell winced. "Well. Anyway, he probably would have kicked me out of the house right then, but Mom started sobbing and begging and appealed to his sense of self-image. A good man wouldn't toss his own son out on the street, you know."

"A good man wouldn't beat up his wife and son."

"You can take that up with him in the afterlife." Lowell drank another sip.

"I think sometimes about how everything played out. Kids were calling me 'fag' in middle school, so I worked my damnedest to appear as straight as possible. That's most of the reason why I took up baseball. You, on the other hand..."

"Yeah, I don't know. I guess I figured that once everyone knew, I might as well go whole hog." Lowell traced a pattern on the bar with his finger. "Part of it was also living up to expectations. I acted like what I thought a gay kid should act like. I was flaming. Crazy clothes, some limp-wristed lisping, and most of it was an act."

"I was going to say, you seem a lot mellower now. Although you still kind of have a way of speaking...it's probably more from you living in the city than anything else. You talk kind of fast."

"I know." Lowell gestured to himself, then pressed a hand to his chest. "But this is me. I spent a lot of time living up to other people's expectations, and then somewhere along the line, I figured out who I was. I still think probably people see me on the street and go, 'Well, he's definitely...'" Lowell see-sawed his hand. "But I don't know if I care. What's the worst anyone can do to me? I guarantee you my father has already done it." He looked up at Neal. He still wasn't sure if Neal's sexuality was public knowledge. "What about you? What's happened to you since high school?"

Neal shrugged. "I didn't have a big coming out. I told my parents after I graduated from college. It was pretty awkward, but we got through it. Mom will not be heading up a PFLAG chapter anytime soon, but it's okay. Everyone knows, but we don't talk about it. I think that's about all I can ask for. Otherwise, I don't lie when people ask, but I don't really advertise. I figure it's nobody else's business."

"That's fair."

Neal frowned. "Yeah, but this is still Greenbriar. I'll tell you a secret." He took a step forward and put his hand on the bar. "I've been seeing this man for a long time, but he's totally in the closet. It's not, like, an exclusive thing. We've both pursued other things on the side. But this has been going on for years. And most of the time it's really great between us. And there's not a soul in the world who knows about it besides him and me."

"That sucks," said Lowell.

Neal nodded. "He's definitely not ready to come out, though. I think he should, but if I put pressure on him, I'd lose him. And I don't want that, either."

"That's a tough spot to be in."

"Yeah," said Neal. "I asked him, you know, what would he do if I had a relationship with another man? And he told me that it was okay for me to go out with other women but not other men. How stupid is that?"

Lowell scratched his chin. "He's 'not gay,' am I right?"

Neal nodded. "He says I'm the only man he's ever slept with."

"That seems like a long time to be with someone and still keep it a secret. You sure this guy is worth it?"

"Oh he's worth it." Neal glanced at Lowell's lips.

"But you want to give him something to think about?" Lowell looked out the window behind the bar and saw Joanie's car pull up.

"Eh, maybe." Neal leaned on the bar, his body closer to Lowell, and his gaze drifted toward Lowell's mouth again. "I asked him specifically what he would do if I went out with you."

"Because that would be like wearing a rainbow T-shirt."

Neal leaned forward more, close enough for Lowell to feel his breath on his face. "He didn't seem to like the idea."

"You know, someone could come in at any moment." Lowell figured it only fair to warn him.

"I don't know if I care anymore." Neal closed the distance between them and kissed Lowell hard. Lowell thought Neal a decent-looking guy, but he wasn't actually interested. Still, he played along for Neal's sake, putting a hand on the side of Neal's face and leaning into the kiss a little. It was pleasant, if not a cauldron of passion.

Joanie walked in. She whistled. "We-ell, what have we here?"

Neal backed off immediately and looked embarrassed. Lowell looked right at him. "I did warn you," he said softly.

Neal surprised Lowell by laughing.

Joanie rolled her eyes and sat next to Lowell at the bar. She raised her eyebrows.

"Believe it or not," Lowell said, "it's not what you think."

"That's what they all say."

"Neal was just having a fit of rebellion. He's worked it out of his system. Haven't you, Neal?"

"Yeah," he said, grinning. "That was a nice kiss, but I don't think we have a future together after all. No offense."

"None taken."

"Uh-huh," said Joanie. "Well, all right. Neal, darling, fetch me a martini."

Neal went about making the drink. Joanie looked at Lowell, who shook his head. Neal pushed the drink in front of Joanie, who considered it for a moment before taking a sip. "Not bad."

Joanie thanked Neal and pulled Lowell over to a table. They sat facing each other. A few other patrons drifted in to distract Neal, who seemed to have mostly recovered and was being a jovial host. Joanie looked back at Lowell. "So why were you kissing Neal?"

"Partly so you'd catch us."

"Did you know Neal is gay?"

"I've known since high school."

Joanie's eyes widened. "Since high school? Why didn't you ever tell me?"

"It wasn't my place to tell."

"So, wait. I only found out Neal's gay recently. How did you find out in high school? Do you just have excellent gaydar?"

Lowell laughed. "It's been a great benefit to my social life that I can usually pick out the other gay men from a crowd, but alas, this is a skill I've had to cultivate over time. So, as far as Neal is concerned, I guessed."

"You guessed."

"Yeah, it kind of popped into my head that he might be gay when we were making out backstage in between scenes during *The Music Man.*"

Joanie laughed. "Wow, Jesus. The things you find out about your old classmates. You should have told me. I mean, Neal's cute. I had a little bit of a crush on him in high school. It would have been good to know I was wasting my time."

"You and I didn't have conversations like that in high school. I never told you who I had crushes on."

"That's true." Joanie scratched her chin. "So, tell me, Lowell, who was the unrequited love of your high school years? The one boy you coveted but could never have."

Lowell sighed. He didn't even have to think about it. "Jason Midland. Who else?"

"What about Jase?" Neal asked as he brought over menus.

"Lowell had a big fat crush on him in high school."

"Joanie!"

"What?"

"Jase? Really?" asked Neal. He seemed intrigued.

"I will not apologize for it," Lowell said. "He was hot, he was talented, and everybody thought he was the greatest guy to ever walk the halls of Greenbriar High. I was not an exception."

"He sometimes wore red briefs too," Neal said.

Joanie and Lowell both looked at him.

"I was on the baseball team. I'm not... I mean, I wasn't really interested in him at the time, I just...looked."

"I don't blame you," Joanie said. "I would have too. You're right, Lowell, Jase was hot. He's still hot."

"And so very unavailable," Lowell said, "which maybe adds to his appeal."

"Maybe not as unavailable as you'd think," Neal said quietly, before he walked away.

What the hell did that mean?

* * *

Jase was surprised when he spotted Karen trotting across the ball field. She glanced at the diamond where Layla's team was playing before she climbed up the bleachers and sat next to Jase. "Hi," she said.

"Hi." He wasn't really that pleased to see her—or, he was, for Layla's sake, though she could have shown up sooner than the fifth inning—but it was a gorgeous day out, and he was determined not to let her spoil his mood. He was enjoying the afternoon off from work, and he loved to watch Layla play T-ball. It had been Layla's suggestion to go to this T-ball camp through no influence of Jase's.

Karen said, "How are we doing?"

"Layla's team is ahead by a run. She's up next." He pointed to the field.

Layla walked up to the tee, holding the bat as though it weighed eighty pounds. Jase was tickled when her tongue appeared between her lips in concentration. She looked intently at the ball, lifted the bat, and swung hard. The ball shot off the tee and well past all three kids standing in the outfield. Jase jumped to his feet. "Yeah, Layla! Go!"

Layla took off around the bases while the kids in the outfield scrambled to get the ball. They stopped her at third base, but the boy who batted before her ran home. Jase whistled, and Layla looked over at the stands with a huge smile on her face. The other parents cheered and clapped.

Another girl was up next. She hit the ball only hard enough for it to fall a few feet in front of the pitcher, who promptly picked it up and threw it home. The catcher missed and stumbled backward, which gave Layla the room she needed to run home. Jase cheered her the whole way. Karen jumped up and hollered and clapped too.

When Layla went back to the bench that served as the home-team dugout, Jase and Karen sat back down, and Karen said, "When we were at the Bronx Zoo last weekend, Layla mentioned your new neighbor. Someone named Lowell?"

Jase felt himself flush, and he had to work hard to keep his reaction to a minimum. This was becoming a problem, his reaction to Lowell's name whenever anyone mentioned it. He swallowed and said with all the calm he could muster, "Yeah. He and I were friends when we were kids. Isn't that a weird coincidence?"

"That is weird. You don't... I mean, Layla said something..."

"What is it?"

Karen gave him a sidelong glance, then whispered, "You don't *like* him, do you?"

"What did Layla say?"

"Nothing, just that you were friends."

Jase wondered at Karen's intuitiveness. "We *are* friends."

"You had a gay friend in school, didn't you? Besides Neal, I mean."

Jase had never so much as flirted with Neal, but he'd been the topic of a number of arguments when his marriage to Karen was falling apart. Karen didn't like Neal, though whether that dislike came from homophobia, jealousy, or genuine distaste, it was hard for Jase to say. Jase felt a little defiant when he said, "That was Lowell. I mean, he's gay, yes."

Karen frowned. "I don't think it's a good idea for you to spend so much time with him."

Through his teeth, Jase said, "It's not up to you who I spend my time with."

"I don't think he should spend time around Layla."

Jase let out the breath he hadn't realized he'd been holding. "Lowell is gay. He's not a pedophile."

"Still..."

"No. End of conversation."

Karen grunted. "You said when we broke up that you wouldn't expose her to any of it. None of the people you've dated."

"I haven't. I won't. Nothing's going on with Lowell."

She shook her head, not looking like she believed him. "This is my parents' weekend with Layla, right?"

"Yes, I was going to drop her off right after the game."

"I can take her."

Jase nodded and turned his attention back on the game. Layla's team won by two runs. As the kids jumped around to celebrate, Jase and Karen walked over to the diamond. Layla squealed, "Mommy!" and ran over to hug her mother. Karen smiled and returned the hug.

"Great game!" Karen said.

Jase motioned for them to follow him, and they walked together to the parking lot. He helped Layla put her equipment in the trunk of his car, and then she moved to climb through the passenger-side door.

"Hey, Layla, you're coming with me tonight," Karen said. "We're going to Grandma and Grandpa's house."

"We need to run home first so Layla can change and get her stuff," said Jase.

"You drive, I'll follow you," said Karen.

"Yeah, all right."

Layla got in Jase's car, so Jase got in and started it. "You have a good game, kiddo?"

"Yes." She looked out the window for a moment. Karen pulled her car up next to them and waved. Layla waved back but looked uneasily back at Jase. "Do I have to go to Grandma and Grandpa's house?"

"Yes, sweetie. It's their weekend with you."

"I don't want to go. Last time, I had to sleep on the couch."

"Why did you have to sleep on the couch? You didn't tell me that." Jase pulled out of the parking lot and headed toward home. He glanced in his rearview mirror and saw Karen's car behind him.

"Grandma and Grandpa were painting my room," she said.

"That's probably done now, so you won't have to sleep on the couch again."

"I know, but… Grandma and Grandpa's house smells funny."

"Layla, you have to spend time with your grandparents." Saying it made Jase's chest hurt. He would have happily let Layla stay with him that weekend.

"If you and Mommy lived together, I wouldn't have to go to Grandma and Grandpa's house."

Jase came close to having to pull the car over. "I know. I'm sorry, but we can't do that."

"I know, 'cause you got divorced." Layla gazed out the window again. After a minute, she said, "Can Lowell come over for dinner tonight?"

"You have to go to your grandparents'," Jase said.

"Oh yeah."

Jase pulled into his driveway a few minutes later. Layla hopped out of the car. "Can I at least take some of my dolls?"

"Sure. Help me carry your stuff inside, and you can pick a few things to take with you."

Layla took her equipment bag and hoisted it over her shoulder while Jase took her backpack. Karen pulled into the driveway behind them. Everyone went inside. Then Layla threw a fit.

She squealed, she cried, she stomped around the living room. Jase wasn't sure how to calm her down. She said, "I won't go. I don't want to," over and over again.

Karen stepped forward and reached out for Layla, but Layla squirmed away.

"Layla, honey, calm down." said Jase. She cried in response.

"What's the problem?" Karen said

Jase took a step away from Layla. "She's probably just tired. It's been a long day."

"I'm not tired!"

"She doesn't want to go with you," Jase said quietly.

"Why not?" Karen knelt next to Layla and reached out a hand. "Why don't you want to go?"

"I don't want to go to Grandma and Grandpa's house. I want to stay here with Daddy. I don't want to go with you."

Karen frowned. "We'll have fun at Grandma and Grandpa's house. We can play a game or watch a movie."

"No," said Layla. She rubbed her face. "Mommy, I don't want to."

Karen's eyes widened. She ran a hand through her hair. She turned to Jase and glowered at him. "Did you say something about me to her?"

"What? No, of course not. She's just tired. Look, maybe you should just have a seat, let her calm down, then she can go. I have to pack a few of her things anyway." He motioned toward the couch.

Karen managed to coax Layla onto the couch, so Jase ran upstairs and packed a bag of clothes and toys. He looked at the bag, tried to puzzle out how his life had become this, why he was packing a bag of clothes to send his daughter away for the weekend. Layla's words echoed in his head. "*If you and Mommy lived together...*" He sat on Layla's bed and bowed his head forward, trying to collect himself. He hated forcing Layla to do anything, and he hated sending her away that one weekend a month, though he'd made this agreement in good faith, recognizing that Karen's parents deserved to keep Layla in their lives.

Rationally, he knew sending Layla off with Karen was the right thing to do, but his heart still broke a little when he finally managed to get them out the door.

This was his penance, he figured. This whole mess was his fault.

Chapter Six

Lowell was surprised when that familiar sick feeling washed over him as he stood on the stoop to his parents' house. His father no longer lived here, he reminded himself. The Old Man wouldn't be waiting inside. It was hard to shake his nerves, but he steeled himself and rang the doorbell. His mother answered it and smiled. "Lowell," she said. "This is your house too. You don't have to ring the doorbell."

"I don't live here anymore," he said.

"It's still your house. It will always be your house. Thank you for coming for lunch." She lit a cigarette. "I made a roast beef."

He followed her into the house. "Mom, you know I don't eat red meat."

"Oh dear." She walked into the kitchen. "I completely forgot. I might have some sliced turkey in the fridge, if you'd rather eat a sandwich."

"That will be fine." He watched his mother shuffle around the kitchen. He remembered a thousand family dinners with her bustling about, his father sitting expectantly at the head of the table, waiting to be fed. The house looked the same, as cluttered as always, as if Old Man Fisher were still around. Lowell hated that he kept expecting his father to jump out from behind the corner, to come down the hall from the master bedroom with a belt in his hand, to materialize on the couch in front of the TV.

"How are you?" he asked.

She stubbed out the cigarette in an ashtray on the counter. "I'm all right." She pulled things out of the fridge. "It's been tough, you know."

Lowell reflected on the relief he'd felt when the call had come telling him his father had died. He couldn't imagine that his mother wouldn't have felt the same.

As if she read his thoughts, she said, "I know you think I'm better off without your father, and maybe I am, but I lived with him for almost forty years."

Lowell felt a tinge of regret. The complicating factor, of course, was that over the years, Lowell's father had cut his mother off from most of her friends, and now she had few people left who she could talk to. He imagined she was lonely. He'd often worried that he'd handled the situation selfishly, that he'd abandoned her to the Old Man in order to save himself. "I'm sorry I haven't been around much," he said.

"It's all right. I know you had your big life in the city."

"Well, now I have the house here, so I'm close by. I'll visit more often. You should come by and see the new place sometime. I don't have much furniture yet, but after I get a few more jobs, I plan to rectify that."

His mother walked over and ran a hand along his back. "I'd be happy to come see your house. Now eat!" She pushed him into a seat at the kitchen table. She fetched a platter from the counter, at the center of which was the roast, surrounded by boiled carrots and potatoes. She sat down and said, "Dig in." She smiled.

"Uh, I'll just go get the turkey from the fridge."

"What are you talking about? I made this nice roast."

Lowell looked at her. "You okay, Mom?"

"Yes, I'm fine." She squinted at him for a moment. "Oh the turkey sandwich."

"I'll do it," he said. He got up and dug through the assorted cold cuts she'd put on the counter until he found the turkey. When he sat back down, he saw that his mother had filled his plate with everything but the meat.

"You don't eat enough, Lowell. You're too thin."

He shook his head. "Thanks, Mom."

* * *

Jase was mowing his front lawn when he saw Lowell's car pull up. He thought about what Karen had said to him the day before, about what they'd agreed to when she'd signed over custody. He had promised he'd never expose Layla to anyone he dated. That was easy enough to stick to when he was going to the city for one-night stands. Not so easy if he got involved in an actual relationship, let alone one with his neighbor, someone Layla saw a few times a week. Not that he was in a relationship with Lowell or had any indication that Lowell was even interested. That was the mystery Jase had spent a lonely night trying to work out. He wasn't sure he really wanted to find out.

Still, he couldn't bring himself to be rude to Lowell. He waved. "Hey neighbor," he shouted.

"Hey," said Lowell as he got out of the car. He trotted over, so Jase cut the engine on the mower.

Jase thought Lowell looked tired. "How are you?"

"I'm...okay. I spent the afternoon with my mother." He shook his head dismissively. "How are you?"

Jase leaned on the mower and sighed. "I'm fine. Layla went to her grandparents' house so I guess I'm a free agent for the rest of the weekend."

"Yeah? You want to go get dinner or something?"

It seemed unwise. There was enough simmering between him and Lowell that Jase knew even just dinner could be a problem. And still he said, "Sure, okay. Let me just finish up here and take a shower. I'll come by in an hour or so?"

Lowell smiled. "Sounds good."

Jase thought it unfair. There was no way he could turn down that face.

So, an hour later, showered and in clean clothes, Jase rang Lowell's doorbell. He was greeted with the smile and the benefit of seeing Lowell in a clean outfit, a dark brown short-sleeved button-down over jeans, and he couldn't help but smile back.

"I was thinking," Jase said, leading Lowell to his car, "that we could go to Dora's."

Lowell paused as he opened the car door and looked at Jase over the roof of the car with confusion. "The take-out pizza place?"

"They opened an adjacent restaurant six years ago. There's plenty of space to sit." The main appeal of the place, though, was that it was casual enough that eating there together wouldn't feel too much like a date. Or so Jase hoped.

They chatted amiably on the drive over to the restaurant, with Lowell quizzing Jase on what else had changed in town. When they got to Dora's, Jase thought it was kind of fun to watch Lowell take in the new place.

They were seated, and Lowell said, "I remember when this opened. That was, what, middle school? And everyone would come by after school for a slice and a soda."

"I remember."

"Joanie and I came in one afternoon when they had just finished making a batch of zeppole. I had never had one before, so I asked what they were, and Dora herself gave me one. We were hooked after that. I think I gained five pounds in zeppole that spring."

Jase chuckled. "Probably you could have used it."

"Probably."

"I remember you being really skinny in high school."

"Scrawny is the word you're looking for."

"But you turned out just fine."

Lowell smiled. "Not without some trial and error. I was vegetarian for a while, most of college actually, but my doctor told me I was too thin and not getting enough protein, so I reintroduced poultry and fish. I still can't eat red meat, though. It just doesn't agree with me." He sighed. "I haven't had any red meat in years, and this afternoon my mother tried to feed me roast beef."

"Does she not approve?"

"No, it's not that. I think she just forgot, which is weird because I haven't eaten red meat in probably fifteen years." Lowell's eyes widened, and he looked, unfocused, at something on the table. "I don't know if she's getting senile or what, but... I mean, this is the reason I moved back to Greenbriar. I'm worried about her."

"Is it possible that she really just forgot, since you haven't been home in a while?"

Lowell scratched his chin. "Yes, I suppose that's possible. I hope that's what it is."

Jase wanted to keep Lowell talking, but they were interrupted by the waitress. Though Dora's menu had grown when the restaurant itself had expanded, the pizza was still the house specialty. They ordered a pie to share, and the waitress left them.

"Speaking of high school," Lowell said. Jase didn't especially want to talk about the past, but he nodded. "I talked to Neal Schusterman a few days ago, and he had some interesting things to say about you."

Jase froze. Neal was probably his closest friend in the world, and there were things they knew about each other that they never spoke of. It seemed unlike Neal to disclose any secrets to Lowell, but Jase was terrified that he had anyway. "What did he say?" Jase tried to sound casual.

Lowell sat back in his chair with a wry smile on his face. "So apparently you used to wear red briefs in high school?"

Jase let out a breath. "I'm going to kill him," he said. He shook his head. "I overheard Alicia Whitborne tell someone that she was dating a guy who wore red briefs, and both girls agreed they were the sexiest things ever, so I went out and bought some. My mother threw a hissy fit, as I recall."

"If only more people could have seen you in your underwear, you would have had all the girls throwing themselves at you." Lowell laughed. "Some of the boys too, I would think."

Jase opted to ignore that. "I was fifteen, what do you want?"

Lowell regarded him carefully. "You're not surprised that Neal noticed your underwear?"

"We saw each other in our underwear every damn day during the baseball season. So my having red ones would have been noticeable." At Lowell's raised eyebrow, Jase added, "I know he's gay. I guess I don't begrudge him sneaking a look."

"I can't imagine how hard it must have been to be a gay athlete."

Jase found himself nodding. "Nobody knew then." When he looked at Lowell, Lowell's brows were furrowed. Jase realized he hadn't been speaking just of Neal and suspected Lowell knew it too.

His panic attack was postponed by the waitress, who brought them their food. Both men helped themselves. Lowell took a bite and moaned. "I forgot how good this pizza was. Better even than the place near my apartment in the Lower East Side."

"Really?"

"Oh yeah."

They ate in contemplative silence for a while. Lowell finished off a slice and took a second. He looked like he wanted to say something.

"What?" Jase asked.

"Nothing. I just…" He looked off into the distance. Then he blinked and refocused his attention back on Jase, which Jase found unsettling at first. Trying to gain control over his own composure, he looked right back at Lowell. Their eyes met. Jase understood in that moment that it was futile to keep secrets from Lowell.

Jase looked away. Lowell *knew*.

"So," Lowell said conversationally, picking some cheese off his pizza.

Jase wanted to deflect attention from the elephant that had just landed in the middle of their table. "This is great pizza." *Well, that was lame.*

"Neal said some other things too. A few offhand comments that I didn't quite know how to interpret. I think I understand what he meant now."

"What did he say?"

Lowell looked down at his plate. "Eh, nothing. Something about you being available. For dating, I mean."

The panic sat like a rock in Jase's chest. "Well, sure, I guess. I'm single, technically. I haven't really wanted to date much since the divorce, though."

"I thought it would be rude to ask you about why your marriage ended, but I have to say, I'm really curious."

"Oh, well, you know." Jase tried to keep his breathing even. "We weren't really right for each other."

"How long was it before your wife left you that you stopped sleeping with her?"

Horrified, Jase sat back in his chair. Lowell kept eating as if he'd just asked Jase about the weather. Jase tried to cover his loss of composure by reaching for a slice of pizza, but his hands shook. Lowell glanced up and saw the movement. Jase dropped his hands into his lap and took a deep breath. "Almost a year," he said quietly.

"She hung in there longer than I would have."

Jase wanted with everything he had to get his breathing back to normal. "Yeah."

Lowell's face fell. "God, I am so sorry. I'm an asshole. I shouldn't have said anything."

Jase rubbed his eyes. "No, it's fine."

"It's not. I was irritated. I took it out on you."

"It's okay."

Lowell sighed. "You want to get out of here?"

"Yeah."

Lowell signaled for the check and paid for dinner before Jase could even get it together enough to reach for his wallet. They had the rest of the pizza packed up to go. Lowell led the way out to Jase's car and volunteered to drive.

"I don't think so," said Jase, pulling his keys out of his pocket.

Lowell slid into the passenger seat. "Are you one of those 'no one drives my car but me' guys?"

"No, but I've seen you drive."

Lowell laughed, which pretty effectively broke the tension. Jase put the car in gear. Lowell did an admirable job keeping the mood upbeat, making small talk and pointing out interesting things they passed on the way. "Oh hey, the bowling alley is still open," he said as they passed Ten Pin Alley. "You had your ninth or tenth birthday party there, right?"

"Yeah. Didn't everyone?"

Lowell shook his head. "My old man was not much for bowling. I always wanted to have a party there, but I think it was mostly because everyone else had their parties there. Either way, my parents never let me."

"We should go sometime."

"Okay. I'll warn you that I'm a terrible bowler."

"I am too. You know, Layla's birthday is coming up. She turns seven right before school starts."

"Wow. Do you have big plans for her birthday?"

"Not yet. Probably there will be a party." A party to which he'd want to invite Lowell but would have to invite Karen. He could fool himself into rationalizing that he didn't know what all this meant, but he did, and it terrified him.

He pulled the car into his driveway.

Lowell said, "I really am sorry about before. Do you want to come over for a cup of coffee? Maybe finish the rest of this pizza?" When Jase looked over at him, Lowell was holding up the box and grinning adorably.

He knew it was a mistake, but he said, "Okay." It felt like even more of a mistake to cross the threshold into Lowell's house, like doing so was putting him past some point of no return, but then his stomach grumbled.

Lowell looked devastated. "You're still hungry."

Jase pointed to the pizza box. "You're holding the food."

"I feel awful. It was terrible of me to end dinner so abruptly. I shouldn't have said anything."

"Stop apologizing. I told you it was fine." When Lowell continued to pout, Jase said, "Heat me up a slice of pizza, and all will be forgiven."

"Done," Lowell said, walking into the kitchen.

Jase observed that Lowell had kind of a swishy way of walking, and he liked the way Lowell's hips moved. Then he realized that he'd been staring at Lowell's butt, so he shook his head and followed Lowell into the kitchen.

Lowell put the pizza box on the counter and opened the lid. "Maybe it's better cold?"

Jase moved around him and took a slice from the box. "Yeah, I think microwaving it changes the taste. Pizza is never as good reheated."

"Cold it is," Lowell said with a smile. "I'll put on a pot of coffee."

Jase devoured his slice of pizza, realizing he was ravenous, and reached for another. As Lowell got the coffee going, he reached for a piece of pizza and stood leaning against the counter as he ate, his face nearly ecstatic as he enjoyed the food.

And Jase couldn't keep himself from thinking about other ways to bring that look to Lowell's face.

Lowell poured two cups of coffee and handed one to Jase. As they sat at the kitchen table, Lowell knocked his own coffee cup into his lap.

"Holy Jesus!" He immediately scooted back in the chair. He stood and grabbed a wad of paper towels and pressed them to his pants.

"Are you okay? Can I get you some ice or something?"

Lowell grunted. "It's okay. I'd make a sterility joke, but it's not like I'm going to father children anytime soon, so…" He tossed the paper towels in the trash and surveyed the damage. "Um, I'm going to go upstairs and change. Sit tight and enjoy the pizza."

Jase tried to sit at the table. He counted to ten before standing and then went up the stairs. Lowell was at the end of the hall, pawing through towels in a linen closet. Jase gave up on resisting and walked to Lowell, who turned around. His eyebrows rose.

Jase approached and trapped him against the wall, putting a hand on either side of his head. Jase was acutely aware of the proximity of their bodies, of Lowell's essential maleness: his scent, his texture, the warmth of his body, the dark stubble along his chin, his Adam's apple. Lowell looked at Jase, his brow furrowed and his lips pursed, but he didn't say anything.

"I don't want to be this way," Jase said, knowing beyond anything how attracted he was to this man he had trapped against the wall.

"I know."

"But I am. I can't pretend otherwise."

"I know that too." He leaned his head back against the wall. "Your wife was the last woman you slept with?" At Jase's nod, Lowell said, "But you've had sex since your divorce. That's math even I can do."

"I've spent a lot of time the last couple of weeks talking myself out of wanting you." He grabbed one of Lowell's hands and placed it on his crotch. "As you can see, that's not going so well."

Lowell gently traced his fingers along the length of Jase's very hard cock through his jeans. "Yeah," he said breathlessly. "I know a little about that. But I was talking myself out of wanting you because I was convinced you were straight."

"Surprise." Jase thrust his hips forward against Lowell's hand. Lowell's touch felt so good but he wanted more, wanted skin-to-skin contact. He put his hands on Lowell's chest and ran his palms down to his firm and flat stomach. Then he looked Lowell in the eye and undid the top button on his jeans.

"God, Jase," Lowell said, leaning forward to kiss him.

Jase thrust his head back to avoid the kiss. "I don't kiss."

"I do," he said, and pulled Jase's head close before smashing their lips together.

It was unlike any kiss Jase had ever experienced. He'd never kissed another man before, though there had been moments when he'd wanted to. It was too intimate, he'd always reasoned. He realized now it had been a wise decision, because his heart pounded as he opened his mouth to accept the kiss.

Lowell's lips were firm and insistent, and Lowell's stubbly face scratched against his own chin. Lowell tasted of pizza and coffee and something else unique to him. It was different from kissing a woman, Jase thought, as the air around him seemed to flood with the smell of Lowell, sweet and masculine. As they kissed, Jase felt something fall into place, felt a rightness to the way their lips fit together.

Lowell pushed him away from the wall and into the bedroom. They kept kissing as Lowell pushed Jase toward the bed. The backs of Jase's legs hit the edge of the mattress, and he toppled backward. He landed on an unmade bed covered in black jersey sheets, soft and smelling of Lowell, of his woodsy shampoo, of his musky *je ne sais quois.*

Lowell looked unsure of how to proceed, so Jase got started by taking off his own shirt. Now that everything was on the table, he couldn't stop himself. He had to have Lowell.

Lowell stood at the foot of the bed and mimicked Jase's movement, his long body stretching as he pulled his shirt off over his head. Lowell's torso was nearly hairless and not as defined as Jase's, but it was enticing just the same. The top button of his coffee-stained jeans was still open.

"Come here," Jase said.

Lowell pushed Jase down on the bed and knelt on the mattress. Jase practically strained toward Lowell.

Jase said, "I have wanted you from the moment I set eyes on you again, that day you moved in."

Lowell's eyes widened at that. "Me too. It feels like I've wanted you my whole life." He crawled over to Jase and hovered over him, propping his upper body up on his hands.

Then he bent his head and kissed Jase again, sucking on his lower lip. "How do you want me?" Lowell asked.

Jase knew but had to close his eyes before he could say it out loud. "Inside me. I want you inside me."

Lowell groaned. He pressed his still-clothed erection against Jase's hip. "I want that too, but…"

Not understanding the hesitancy, Jase opened his eyes and looked at Lowell, whose face was flush. He put his hands on either side of Lowell's beautiful face. "So do it."

"Trust me, I would love nothing better, but I don't have any condoms here. I never expected to get laid in Greenbriar."

"Oh," said Jase.

Lowell leaned down and planted wet kisses along Jase's cheek, along his jaw. "That doesn't mean we can't…" He pushed his jeans down his hips. He helped Jase out of his jeans, and their bodies pressed together, giving Jase the contact he craved. Lowell's body was warm and a little sweaty, and they seemed to slide together easily. Jase ran his hands over Lowell's back, savoring the feel of all that smooth skin. Lowell hooked a finger into Jase's underwear. "Not red briefs," he said, tugging the gray boxer-briefs down Jase's thighs.

"I've still got a pair, if that interests you."

Lowell grinned. "Very much." He kissed the place where Jase's neck met his shoulder and wiggled out of his own briefs. Jase realized with some surprise that he was naked and in bed with Lowell Fisher, and the power of his wanting rushed through his veins. He groaned as Lowell's cock rubbed against his own, smooth and hard and hot.

Lowell pressed the full length of his body against Jase. Jase's back arched, and his skin broke out in goose bumps everywhere. Lowell kissed him hard and thrust his hips, and Jase felt overwhelmed, surrounded by the scent of Lowell, by the presence of his body, by the intensity of the sensation of their bodies moving together. He groaned, which encouraged Lowell to press harder against him.

Lowell kissed and nipped at his shoulder, and with his fingers traced long, lazy paths down Jase's arms. Jase touched Lowell's shoulders and slid his hands down the whole length of Lowell's back, which was smooth, strong, and slick with sweat. He reached for Lowell's ass, and he moved his hands over it before cupping a cheek in each hand. Lowell had a fantastic ass, round and perfectly shaped. Jase pulled it closer to him, to better rub their cocks together. Little shocks ran through his body every time he felt the head of Lowell's cock slide against his own. He leaned up and kissed Lowell and everything bloomed, pleasure pulsing through his body.

Lowell lifted his head and looked Jase in the eyes. His expression made it seem like he might be in pain, but he said, "I'm not going to last long. This is too good."

"Yes," Jase said, thrusting against Lowell, his own orgasm building.

Lowell let out a long groan and pumped his hips once more. Hot, wet spurts splashed on Jase's chest and belly. The pulse of Lowell's cock against his triggered Jase's orgasm. He dug his fingers into Lowell's shoulders and thrust against him a few more times before he closed his eyes and surrendered.

The intensity of the orgasm surprised him and stole his breath as he pumped against Lowell.

Lowell, he thought as he came back down. He was in Lowell's arms, in Lowell's bed, as if he belonged there. He pulled Lowell close to him and held him there, needing to know Lowell was really there, that this wasn't just some crazy dream.

Lowell kissed him, and he knew it wasn't a dream. Lowell was too real, too present. The room smelled of musky man and sex, an intoxicating combination. Plus he felt their mixed cum start to dry on his belly.

Lowell sat up. "Don't go anywhere." As soon as he was out of the bed, Jase missed the weight on top of him. Lowell soon returned, though, with a wet cloth in his hand. He cleaned them both up, then vanished back into the bathroom.

When he returned this time, he slid into bed next to Jase and pulled the sheets over them. "You don't kiss," he said. "Who do you think you are, Julia Roberts?"

Jase had to look away. "I didn't want to share that kind of intimacy with my one-night stands."

"Jase," Lowell said. Jase turned. "I'm not some stranger. We've known each other too long. We're friends, right? I deserve better than to be treated as a one-off. Don't I?"

"Yes." Jase sighed. "And I really like kissing you."

Lowell smiled. "Good." He kissed Jase lazily, running a hand through Jase's hair. "We should probably clean up downstairs. I think I left the coffeemaker on, and the pizza will attract bugs."

"You are really good at the romantic pillow talk," Jase said, laughing.

"Will you stay the night? I want you to stay the night."

Jase thought about his house next door, sitting completely empty. The prospect of spending the rest of the night alone was not a happy one. "Yes. I would love to stay."

Chapter Seven

Lowell sat on the swing set in Jase's backyard, swinging gently. He watched the back of the house, watched lights come on and go off in the windows. Jase had gone inside to tuck in Layla, which gave Lowell a little too much time to contemplate the fact that this man he was getting involved with had a child. It was one thing to be friends with someone with a daughter, but if they became romantically involved, what would that mean for Lowell? Would he be expected to take care of her? Be responsible for her? Or was it too early in their relationship—if it could even be called that, since all they'd done was sleep together last night—to think about it?

Jase tumbled back out of the back door and grinned. He walked over to the swing set and sat down on the swing next to Lowell, facing the other way.

"Layla all put to bed?" Lowell put his thoughts aside and put some effort into smiling.

"Yep. She was exhausted. I bet she's already asleep."

Lowell nodded and started using his feet to rock back and forth on the swing. "You remember coming out here late at night when we were kids?"

"Of course." Jase kicked his feet at the dirt.

Lowell felt Jase watching him. He stopped moving the swing. "So."

"So."

Lowell looked at Jase, feeling the same sense of wonder he'd felt when they'd fallen into bed the night before. Jase was so handsome, his hair tossed around a little by the wind, his expression pensive. "I guess I know now why your marriage fell apart."

"Yeah," Jase said, looking out into the woods behind his house. "Karen knew. I think she always knew, right from the beginning. I think she loved me enough that she overlooked it. She wanted to be with me anyway, or thought I'd get over it. I don't know. I did genuinely care about her. We were good friends once. We had a lot of fun together when we were in college. So when she started hinting that she wanted to get married, I talked myself into agreeing. And I could do it, you know, I could make love to her, and it was fine."

"But then you stopped."

"I wasn't attracted to her. I mean, obviously I wasn't. When sex started to feel more like going through the motions than any expression of affection. That's when I backed off."

"But you couldn't leave her."

"I did like her." He sighed. "But, yeah, leaving was like failure. If she left me, it wasn't my fault the marriage ended. Obviously, that's not true, but that's what I told myself."

Lowell nodded. "When did you know?"

Jase shook his head. "When did I know I was gay?" He barely whispered the last word. "I'm not really sure."

"But you knew before you met Karen."

"Yeah."

Lowell didn't find that surprising. He figured that being married to a woman probably also eased some of his self-hatred. What had he said the previous night? *I don't want to be this way.* Lowell was reluctant to pry too much, but he'd also stumbled upon a treasure. He wanted to keep Jase talking but didn't want to piss him off. "If you feel uncomfortable, feel free to tell me to shut the hell up. I don't mean to push you. I'm just... I'm fascinated. Never in a million years would I have guessed, and last night was so surreal. I'm still not sure it happened."

"It happened," Jase said. "And this is okay. It feels good to talk about it. I've wanted to tell you for so long, and I just...couldn't."

"You fooled me with the whole marriage thing."

"I know. I fooled myself. I thought I could do it, I really did. I mean, men are supposed to be with women. That's how the world works. It took me a long time to figure out that I couldn't make *me* work that way." Jase picked up a rock and hurled it at a tree with all the precision of a major-league first baseman. It hit the tree with a *thock.* "It was Karen who made me give up baseball. I mean, I never would have played for the Yankees, but I think I could have made it to a decent team in the minors. But we wanted to have kids. I wanted to have kids, right from the beginning, and Karen said life as a professional baseball player would be too unpredictable. And she was right. I could have gotten traded and sent across the country, or I could have gotten injured and then been totally unemployable."

Jase's sorrow radiated off him. Lowell wondered at a man making the choices Jase had made. He'd given up the thing he'd most wanted for marriage, and he'd gotten married because he couldn't accept that he was gay.

Before Lowell could say anything, Jase said, "I'd do it again. We had Layla after all. I love Layla more than I've ever loved anything, and I want to get it right. I want her to be happy and healthy, and I'd do whatever it takes to make sure that happens."

"Even if it meant sacrificing yourself?"

"Isn't that what I've already done?"

Lowell couldn't decide if he should pity Jase for his losses or admire him for his devotion to his daughter. He couldn't formulate a response, didn't know how he should react. They swung in silence for a while.

Jase said, "There was a night, kind of like this one, when we were maybe thirteen? It was hot. It was definitely during the summer. I think we'd done something together that day, like maybe we went down to the pool at the Y, and then you came over for dinner."

"I don't remember," Lowell said, wishing he did, wondering where Jase was going with this little trip down memory lane.

Jase didn't seem to hear him. "We were sitting out here on the swings, just like this, talking about whatever, probably baseball." Jase kicked a rock, and it flew through the air into the darkness. "I don't remember what it was, but I do remember looking over at you and thinking, 'I really like looking at Lowell.'" He shook his head. So quietly that Lowell could barely hear, he added, "Just looking at you made me happy. Something about your face, but more than that, at that moment, I looked at you, and I got hard. And at first, you know, I thought, I'm just pumped up because we had a busy day, we were having fun, but no, it was you." He cleared his throat. "I think I made you go home after that, like I made up an excuse about having to do something early the next morning, and you left. Then I freaked right the hell out."

"That's when you knew."

"Pretty much."

"And that's why you stopped talking to me."

"I'm not like you, Lowell. What you did in high school, that was so brave. I was a coward. I'm still a coward."

"I always thought—or I told myself—that we'd just drifted apart. I only ever followed baseball because you loved it, so when you started spending all of your time with your teammates, and I started doing more art and theater, I figured, well, that's how it goes. People grow up and grow apart."

"I couldn't be around you anymore."

"There were other boys, though. Ones you were attracted to, I mean."

Jase twisted in the swing, creating a double helix with the chains. "Oh sure. Baseball practice was torture, as you've already guessed. Everyone in the locker room after practice, all those male bodies, sweaty and smelly, and I was in heaven and hell at the same time. I loved to look, and I hated that I loved to look. But that was one thing. Being with someone, being in a relationship with a guy, that didn't ever seem possible. I conjured all these worst-case scenarios in my head. My parents would disown me, I'd get kicked off the team, no one would like me anymore."

"Yeah," Lowell had had all those thoughts too. And his father practically had disowned him. "Jase?"

Jase stopped rotating his swing. He picked up his feet and let the chains untwist, and he spun with them. When the swing hung straight again, he looked at Lowell. "Karen calls me Jason, you know. When I got to college, I went by Jason."

"Which do you prefer?"

"Jase. I like the way you say it. It reminds me that I knew you when I was called Jase."

Lowell smiled. "I want you to know that it means a lot that you are willing to talk to me."

Jase smiled back. "Yeah."

Lowell contemplated the ground for a moment. "Were there other men? Before Karen?"

"No," said Jase. "I couldn't…"

"But since?"

Jase bowed his head. "You can't fight nature, I guess."

"Jase?"

Jase looked at him.

Lowell leaned over and touched Jase's face lightly with his hand, then leaned in for a kiss. It was light and tender and then deepened into something with more promise. Lowell thought of what Jase had just said, about Jase looking at Lowell and getting hard, and Lowell understood that, sitting on those swings with an erection so hard it hurt. He deepened the kiss, which was met enthusiastically, but then Jase interrupted and said, "We can't… Layla's upstairs." They kept kissing, though.

"When can you make some time?" Lowell dared to hope this wouldn't play out to be just long talks in Jase's backyard. Was it fair to expect more than that? Was that what dating someone with a kid really meant? Being chaste when the kid was around, even though his fingers itched to touch Jase whenever they were near each other? Hiding and pretending they weren't involved? Lowell wondered if he could do that, if it would be worth it in the long run.

Jase kissed him again. For someone without much experience kissing men, Jase was incredibly talented at it.

Oh it's worth it, Lowell thought.

"Layla's having dinner with Karen on Thursday. Assuming Karen actually shows up, I could give you a couple of hours then."

"I'll take it."

* * *

Karen called Jase at work the next day. He ignored the chirp of his cell phone the first time, but when it rang again ten minutes later, he grabbed it and ran down the hall. There was no way he could have a private conversation from his cubicle, but his office building had a little anteroom near the lobby from which he could at least talk to her without interruption or people around to overhear.

"Karen, I'm at work," he said when he answered the phone.

"I hate to even ask this," she said, which Jase knew was a lie. "But I was wondering if I could borrow some money."

Jase rubbed his forehead and leaned against a wall. "For what?" He did a mental run through his finances, trying to calculate what he could afford to give her, though as he did so, he grew angry. Something in him snapped. Maybe it was the tone she'd asked him with, maybe it was because this was the third or fourth time she'd asked him for money in the last two months, but suddenly, he was no longer willing to just fork it over.

"I need to make a payment on my car," she said, "but also, I thought I'd take Layla somewhere nice when we go to dinner on Thursday."

The last time Karen had borrowed money to "do something nice for Layla," she'd spent at least half of it on herself. And besides, "borrow" was a relative term. Jase knew he'd never see any of that money again.

"Forget it," Jase said.

"What?"

"I'm not lending you any more money. You know, I have custody of our daughter. By rights *you* should be paying *me* child support."

"Come on, Jason, you know I don't have any money."

"I know! Of course I know that!" When he realized he was shouting, Jase took a deep breath. "Look, I don't have a lot to give you right now. I'm paying for Layla's T-ball camp. I'm going to have to buy new school clothes next month. I appreciate that you want to do something nice for Layla, but you know that she'd probably be happier eating pizza than she would be eating at some fancy-pants restaurant. And your car payments are not my problem."

"You've never had a problem loaning me money before."

"I'm sorry. I just can't. Maybe your parents can help." He was proud that he could sound so calm. The longer the call lasted, the more he vibrated with anger.

"So what's changed? You aren't dating someone, are you?"

"What? No, of course not." The thought passed through his mind that he would have been under no obligation to tell Karen even if he were. He didn't think he was, though. A couple of meals out and one night spent together didn't really constitute "dating," did it?

"I'd hate to find out you were dating some woman—or, God forbid, a man—from one of my friends, you know? You'd tell me, right?"

"I...yeah, I'd tell you."

"Because my friend Julie said she thought she saw you at Dora's the other night with some guy."

The bottom fell out of Jase's stomach. It took him a moment longer than was probably appropriate while he weighed whether it was better to lie—to say, "Nope, wasn't me," and have this conversation be over—or to tell the truth. He settled on, "I'm allowed to have a social life. I had pizza with one of my buddies. What's the big deal?"

"So it's okay for you to go out, but you don't have enough money to loan me?"

Jase supposed "he paid" would make it sound too much like a date. "You know what? This is ridiculous. I don't have to justify myself to you. I've already loaned you more than a thousand dollars since the beginning of June. I'm not a fucking bank."

Karen was silent for so long that Jase thought she'd hung up. He was about to check when she said, "Frankly, Jason, I don't like the person you've become lately."

He sighed. "When are you picking Layla up on Thursday?"

He managed to make arrangements, then got Karen off the phone. He walked back to his cubicle feeling defeated. He took small comfort in having narrowly won this battle, but he knew he hadn't won the war.

Chapter Eight

Lowell walked up to Schuster's. Neal stood at the top of a ladder, scrubbing at some graffiti under the bar's big overhead sign. On closer inspection, Lowell saw that the graffiti made the sign read SCHUSTER'S A FAG. "That's charming," Lowell said.

"Just high school kids." Neal scrubbed at a big purple f. "This happens every six months or so. The kids in town seem to think they need to remind me I'm a big 'mo." He grunted and climbed down the ladder. "I'm gonna have to paint over that. They used the fucking oil-based shit."

Lowell followed Neal into the bar. He sat on a stool while Neal went into the back room and reappeared again with a can of paint. "Do you have paint on hand just for this purpose?"

Neal shrugged. "Like I said, they do this every six months or so."

"You want help?"

"No, I can do it." Neal started to walk back toward the door. "Well, on second thought, maybe you could hold the ladder for me."

"Sure."

Lowell spotted Neal while Neal painted over the graffiti. When he was done, Lowell helped him carry the ladder back around to the back of the building. "I'd buy you a beer," Lowell said, "but that seems silly if you own the bar."

Neal laughed. "Yeah. Thanks, by the way. The last time I had to paint over graffiti, I nearly killed myself when wind rocked the ladder."

"Not a problem."

"Come in, and I will buy *you* a drink."

Lowell followed Neal back inside. He sat at the bar and ordered a club soda, which Neal began preparing by plunking a generous slice of lime on the rim of the glass.

"What brings you here?" Neal asked.

Lowell held up his messenger bag. "I was actually hoping to commandeer one of your tables for a couple of hours. I've got a bunch of work to do, but sitting at home was getting too distracting. It's too quiet." He took a sip of his soda. "I'm still kind of adjusting to working as a freelancer. It's strange not to have an office to go to every day."

"But nice too, right? I got a job as an office drone right out of college, and I was only too happy to leave it when my grandfather offered me the bar."

"It is nice."

"Well, any time you want to come use a table here, you're welcome."

"Thanks, Neal. Any time you need help cleaning up graffiti, give me a call."

"Don't say things like that. I'll hold you to it."

"I was serious," said Lowell. He surveyed the space and decided a table in the back corner, near a window, would be the ideal place to work. "Is it always the same, the graffiti?"

"Variations on a theme. 'Fag' seems to be a favorite, but I think last time they wrote, 'Schuster's a big fat queer,' and one time, 'Schuster's a cocksucker,' with an accompanying illustration which my mother saw and was duly traumatized by."

"Lovely."

"It's Greenbriar. That's how it is. I'd move, but I love this bar."

"This town," Lowell said, shaking his head. "I knew I moved away for a reason."

Neal laughed bitterly. "Welcome home, Lowell."

* * *

After Karen picked up Layla on Thursday, Jase immediately headed next door. As he rang the doorbell, it occurred to him that having a prearranged booty call took some of the magic out of it, but he'd wanted Lowell for so long that he didn't care anymore.

Lowell answered the door with a half smile on his face. "Hello, sexy," he said. "Come on in."

Now that he was standing in Lowell's doorway, there was no denying the reality of the situation. Jase was suddenly nervous. "Karen's taking Layla to the Tex-Mex place in Danbury. I think I can give you two hours."

"That should be adequate," Lowell said with an eye roll as he headed for the stairs.

Jase liked that there was no pretense here, that they both knew exactly what was about to happen. But still Jase hesitated, as if he could postpone the inevitable. He wasn't sure why he resisted Lowell, but suddenly it felt like his feet had been trapped in cement. When Jase remained at the foot of the stairs, Lowell said, "Are you just going to stand there?"

"I'm coming." Jase slowly followed Lowell up the stairs.

Lowell went into his bedroom, pulling his T-shirt off as he walked. Jase watched Lowell's muscles move, stretching and straining as Lowell tossed the shirt at his hamper. Jase's fingers tingled, and he wanted to get his hands on all that skin, to touch all that muscle and sinew.

Lowell turned around and smiled, motioning for Jase to move closer. Jase closed the space between them and put his hands on Lowell's bare shoulders, pressing his palms down. Lowell's skin was firm and smooth and wonderful to touch. Lowell put his hands on Jase's waist, then leaned down and kissed him. The kiss was soft but full of promise, and Jase felt the last of his defenses melt away. He marveled at how much he liked kissing Lowell, how there was nothing about it that felt strange or unnatural. He opened his mouth and let Lowell in, made their tongues tangle.

"Mmm," said Lowell against Jase's mouth. "I've been thinking about you all day." He pressed his erection against Jase's hip.

Jase groaned. Knowing that Lowell had been thinking about him was an incredible turn-on. "I've been thinking about you all week."

Lowell put his arms around Jase and pulled their bodies tight together. He laughed. "Who needs foreplay? Let's just get naked."

Jase kissed Lowell again. He wondered why he'd ever thought to deprive himself of the thrill of kissing Lowell. "I want you to fuck me."

"I'm on it." Lowell pushed Jase toward the bed. As he maneuvered Jase, he laughed again. "There's a part of me that still can't believe this." He nibbled at Jase's neck. "I had fantasies about this moment when I was a teenager."

Jase frowned at him. Was he just Lowell's teenage fantasy? "We're adults now, though. It's different."

Lowell jerked away a little. "Yes, it is different. That was teenage lust. This is you and me, and everything that's happened since. I feel like I've gotten to know the real you since I moved back to Greenbriar."

Jase wondered if he knew himself even, but he let it go, knowing there was some truth to Lowell's pronouncement, knowing that he, himself, had gotten to know Lowell and liked him immensely. Even the lust was different now than it had been as a teenager. He'd looked at Lowell and felt happy and aroused, but now there was something else entirely going on, and Lowell was a fully-realized adult with a mature body.

Jase ran his palm up the planes of Lowell's chest. He dipped his head and licked the space between Lowell's pecs. The skin there tasted salty. He inhaled that heady combination of sweet sweat and metallic masculinity. Lowell shuddered under his hands. Lowell laced his fingers through his hair, then gently pulled his head back up and met him with a kiss that made his knees weak.

"I left the condoms in the bathroom," Lowell said. "Sit tight for a moment."

Lowell slipped out the door, so Jase went about taking his clothes off. When he was naked, he climbed on the bed on his hands and knees and waited.

Lowell come back in the room, and a strangled gasp came out of his mouth. "Oh man," he whispered. "Turn around."

Jase turned his head back to look at Lowell. "What?"

Lowell came around the side of the bed, undoing his pants as he got there. He set the box of condoms on the side table. He patted Jase's ass. "It's not that I don't enjoy the view," he said, "because, holy mother, you have a great ass. But I am not fucking you for the first time from behind. Roll over. I want you on your back."

Jase was surprised, but he complied, rolling over onto his back, keeping his gaze on Lowell as much as he could. Lowell slid off his pants and briefs, and Jase finally got a good look at him. His body was amazing, all lean muscle and straight lines. It stirred things in Jase, every movement making his breath catch.

Lowell reached into his drawer and produced a bottle of lube. He leaned down, and they kissed. The kiss seemed electrically charged, all sensation going from Jase's lips to his dick. Jase put his hands on Lowell's shoulders and pulled him close, and everywhere their skin touched sizzled. Lowell groaned into Jase's mouth as he reached between his legs. Jase let his legs fall open, craving Lowell's touch, his body already arching off the bed before Lowell had even touched him properly. God, just Lowell's presence there next to him had Jase sweaty and wanton.

Lowell got up on his knees and maneuvered his body so that he could still kiss Jase as he poured lube onto his fingers. He slid a tentative hand over Jase's opening. Just that small touch had Jase jerking and writhing.

Lowell's probing fingers were almost hesitant, and Jase's mind flashed on all the furtive encounters in club back rooms and grody New York City apartments. They'd always been rushed, either because Jase and the other man were so hot and bothered that they couldn't wait or because they were trying to make miracles happen in the few minutes they had. Lowell was behaving now as if they had all the time in the world. Jase wanted to rush this forward out of habit, but he held back, remaining as still as he could as he kissed Lowell, concentrating on that, on the feel of their lips moving together, or the feel of Lowell's smooth skin under his hands.

Lowell mumbled and then pushed at Jase's knees. Jase lifted his legs, which gave better access. Lowell's slick fingers slid over his skin, sending pulses of pleasure through his body, but the anticipation was driving him batty. Lowell continued his tentative exploring, and just when Jase was about to lose patience, Lowell pressed a finger inside.

Lowell's hard cock pressed into his thigh, and he wanted to touch it but couldn't reach without complicating matters. He almost said something, but Lowell added a second finger, and then they were in business.

Jase could hardly believe this was happening. He was amazed that it hardly hurt at all. His lovers had never been especially careful, not so invested in making sure Jase was comfortable, and God knew Karen had never touched him where Lowell was touching him now. But this was Lowell. *Lowell.* A man Jase had known since they were kids. A man who often plagued his thoughts. A man so hot he made Jase crave and want him like he'd wanted no other. And everything Lowell did to Jase made his skin sing, made Jase feel crazy.

Lowell's fingers slid over all those nerve endings, then curled, brushing against Jase's prostate, sending jolts of pleasure up Jase's spine. Lowell continued to press forward carefully, until Jase found himself groaning, "More."

Lowell smiled and then added a third finger. He pumped his hips against Jase's thigh, and Jase felt nearly overwhelmed suddenly, pressed as he was against this very male body. Lowell moved his mouth over Jase's face to kiss his jawline and nibble his earlobe. Lowell's breaths had shortened, meaning he was getting off on this too, that he was as turned on by Jase's body as Jase was by his.

"More," Jase repeated.

Lowell withdrew his fingers and moved away slightly, leaving Jase feeling empty. Jase touched Lowell's hip to try to coax him back. Lowell reached for the box of condoms but seemed content to let Jase touch him, so Jase did, running his hands over Lowell's chest, his hips, then wrapping his hand around Lowell's cock. He looked at Lowell closely and felt how surreal the situation was. Lowell had been his childhood friend, but now he was sitting here naked, now his hard (and, hello, quite large) cock was in Jase's hand. He pushed those thoughts out of his head and tried to treat Lowell as just a man, as any of the many he'd slept with before.

But then Lowell said, "Jase," softly.

That was about Jase's undoing. "I need you," he said, not completing the thought, which was that he needed Lowell touching him, above him, around him, inside him. He took the condom and rolled it on Lowell's cock, then spread his knees in invitation. Lowell shifted on the bed again, finally settling between Jase's legs. He guided his cock toward Jase. Jase gasped when he felt the head pressing against his hole.

"You okay?" Lowell asked.

"Yes. Now. Please. Lowell."

Lowell pushed his hips forward slowly. Lowell's cock was so very much larger than his fingers, but Jase found satisfaction in the searing pain as his body adjusted. Even so, Lowell's slow push frustrated him; he wanted the pleasure he knew this could bring him, and he couldn't understand why Lowell insisted on drawing this out. Did he not want to do this?

Jase looked up at Lowell, whose face showed the effort he was putting into restraining himself. But then he was completely buried in Jase. Jase's body buzzed with anticipation. He reveled in the fullness he felt, in the connection between their bodies. Lowell hooked his arms behind Jase's knees and pressed Jase's legs into his chest. He leaned forward and kissed Jase, trapping Jase's cock between them, and creating a wonderful friction that pulled a groan from Jase and made him arch off the bed again. He murmured Lowell's name like a plea. He needed Lowell to move. Just when Jase didn't think he could take much more, Lowell shifted his hips.

"Oh God," Jase said against Lowell's lips. The reason for Lowell's slow progress was made clear. The pain was gone, and Lowell's body moved against Jase's flesh, making his skin tingle. Heat and sweat and friction concentrated at the point where their bodies met. Lowell moved in and out of him, and the head of Lowell's cock brushed against that bundle of nerves, sending electricity through Jase's body. Jase was worried he'd come right then. He bit his lip and tried to stave off the orgasm.

Lowell groaned and leaned his forehead against Jase's shoulder. Lowell shook with the effort, as if this coupling was undoing him as well. Jase whispered his name and held him close. He lifted his head again and looked at Jase. Their eyes met, but Jase found looking into his eyes to be too intense. Jase kissed him. Lowell hummed as they kissed, the vibrations tickling Jase's mouth. He reached between them, wrapped his hand around Jase's cock, and started to stroke gently. It didn't take much, between the scents and sensations all around Jase, and soon he was coming hard into Lowell's hand, which earned him a grunt and a kiss. Lowell picked up the pace, thrusting faster and harder, groaning the whole time, until suddenly his whole body went stiff, and he held his breath. He let out that breath on a long moan and clutched at Jase, then collapsed on top of him.

"Wow," said Jase.

"I know."

"You were... That was intense."

Lowell was still panting. He lifted his head far enough for Jase to see him grin. "We're clearly going to have to do that again."

Jase found himself laughing. "Oh man." He was conscious of the fact that Lowell was still inside him.

"Although not right now, because I can't really move."

A part of Jase wanted to thank Lowell, to thank him for taking the time to go slow, to thank him for making it feel so good, to thank him just for being Lowell, but he knew that would sound cheesy, so he didn't say anything. He opted to just lie there, wrapped up in Lowell.

That didn't last long though because Lowell sighed and slid out, then rolled off Jase. "Be right back," he said, before disappearing into the bathroom.

Jase was kind of a sticky mess, so he got up and walked toward the bathroom. Lowell had left the door ajar and was standing at the sink, washing his hands. "I think I need a shower," said Jase.

Lowell gave him a long look, running his gaze from his face to his feet and back up again. Jase, to his amazement, started to get hard again. Lowell really was going to be his downfall.

Lowell laughed. "All right. Hit the showers, Midland. I'll help you wash your back."

* * *

The next morning, Lowell was feeling pretty good when he dropped by his mother's house. Jase had ultimately had to go home to his daughter, so they hadn't spent the night together, but Lowell fully intended for Jase's next free weekend to be spent as naked as possible. Jase had a fantastic body, for one thing. He also made these little sounds when Lowell was inside him that had gotten into Lowell's head—just little gasps and yelps of pleasure—and that moment that their eyes had met right before Jase came was an intense one, an image Lowell wouldn't forget anytime soon.

He rang the doorbell and waited. When she didn't come to the door within a minute or two, he tried the knob. It turned without resistance. He went inside. "Mom?"

His mother wandered out from the back of the house. "Lowell. What are you doing here?"

"We have lunch plans."

"Oh." She frowned. "I guess I forgot. I didn't make anything."

"That's all right." He put a hand on her elbow and steered her into the kitchen. "We can go out if you want." His mother still looked vaguely distressed. Lowell guided her toward a chair.

She sat. "How are you? You look like you're feeling pretty well."

"Yeah, I'm all right. I'm kind of in the mood for Asian food. Is that sushi place near the mall still open?"

"I think it is." She rubbed her forehead. "Let me just sit for a moment, then we can go."

"Okay." He wasn't sure what to do. "Can I get you something?"

"Maybe some juice." She looked vaguely confused.

"Are you okay?"

"Yes, I'm fine. Just...a little dizzy. This happens sometimes, but I'll be good in a moment." She offered him a weak smile.

Lowell opened the fridge to find her some juice and saw that there was none. The fridge was surprisingly empty. There were the normal staples like a carton of milk and a half-finished loaf of bread, but he had grown up in a house that always had a fridge brimming over with more food than any three-person family could ever eat. Not to mention that her car keys were sitting on one of the shelves. He supposed he could chalk up the extra real estate to the fact that his mother lived alone now, but there was still something off about all that empty space. "Mom, when was the last time you went grocery shopping?"

"Well, I was going to go yesterday, but I couldn't find my keys. I looked everywhere, practically tore the house upside down, and they were nowhere."

Lowell extracted her keys from the refrigerator and handed them to her. She looked at them with a puzzled expression. "Oh," she said. Then she closed her eyes. "Shit."

These are all definitely bad signs, thought Lowell. "Are you sure you're okay?"

"No."

He sat at the table and took her hand. He waited until she looked up, and their eyes met. She seemed to have come back to herself. "How long has this been going on?"

"I don't know. I mean, I've had some trouble finding things since your father... But I thought it was because he'd misplaced things, and I couldn't ask him where they were. But now that he's been gone for a little while, I don't know."

"Have you seen a doctor?"

"No."

"Maybe you should. I'll make an appointment for you, if you like."

She nodded. They sat together at the table for a long, silent moment, and then she let go of his hand and rubbed his arm. "I'm so happy to have you back. I missed you while you were gone in the city."

"I'm sorry I stayed away as long as I did."

"I know why. That man."

"He's gone now." Lowell said it as much to reassure himself as his mother. The house still felt haunted by the Old Man, still felt like a dangerous place. "Have you considered moving?"

His mother shook her head. "Where would I go?"

Lowell sighed. That was a fair question. "Can I buy you lunch? Maybe getting out of the house for a little while will help you. I'll bring you by the grocery store on the way back."

She stood and nodded. "That would be nice."

Lowell stood too. He put an arm around his mother and steered her toward the door.

Chapter Nine

Lowell was working when the phone rang. Jase responded to his "Hello" with a breathless, "I have a favor to ask and it's a big imposition so it's okay to say no but I would really really appreciate it if you said yes." The sentence came out quickly, in one rapid blurt.

Lowell laughed. "What is it?"

"I have to run into the office, and I need someone to watch Layla. It would just be for a couple of hours, and you don't even have to do anything except stay with her, and—"

"Jase? Are you asking me to babysit?"

Jase let out a breath. "Yeah. Can you?"

"Of course. I'd be happy to."

"Really?"

The truth was that Lowell had never really babysat before, but he was touched that Jase would trust him with his daughter. "Yes, really. When do you need me? Do you mind if I bring some work?"

"Now would be good. Or as soon as you can. Just come over when you're ready. Bringing work is fine. I can pay you for your time."

"No need to pay me. Not in money anyway."

Jase chuckled. "I don't think I want to know what you have in mind."

"Oh it involves nudity. Not appropriate for family hour."

"Oh," said Jase. He was silent for a moment. "Well, I will be sure to thank you profusely at a later date."

As he walked next door with his messenger bag over one shoulder, he thought about what this might mean in the greater scheme of things. It could be a good opportunity to get to know Jase's daughter better, but did that imply that Lowell was putting himself in a position to take on a bigger role in her life? He stopped in Jase's driveway and looked up at the house. Was he ready to take on a bigger role? A wave of panic passed through him. But, he thought, Jase just asked me to babysit. He didn't ask me to be a father. Hell, Jase and I are just…what? Sleeping together? Dating?

He told himself to calm down. This was a friendly favor, not a marriage proposal. He sighed and walked up to the door.

Layla answered it. "Lowell!"

"Hey, kid. You ready for a night of fun and adventure?"

Layla giggled. "Daddy's just going to the office, and you're just going to babysit me. It's not a big deal."

"It is to me," he said. "I've never been a babysitter before. You'll have to tell me how I'm doing."

"Okay."

Jase came out of the kitchen, a briefcase in his hand, a frantic expression on his face. "You are my favorite person right now."

"I get that a lot," Lowell said.

Layla giggled.

"Okay. She's got dolls and coloring books and whatever else in her room." He looked pointedly at Layla. "She knows to put everything away when she's done. But if you just want to put on a movie or something, that's okay too. I should only be two hours or so, but just in case it's later, bedtime is nine. And, uh, we already ate, so you don't need to feed her. Okay?"

"We'll be fine," Lowell said. He was a little intimidated by the prospect of being responsible for a six-year-old girl, but he reasoned that it would be only a few hours. She had struck Lowell as a smart and well-behaved child. He also wanted Jase to think he could handle it.

Jase gave Layla a kiss on the top of her head, then looked Lowell in the eyes for a long moment, then he was gone. Lowell was nervous, but he smiled. "So. What shall we do?"

Layla scrunched up her face in thought. "Um. Do you like to color?"

"I love to color."

"Okay, wait here."

Lowell sat on the couch. While she ran upstairs, he got out the drawings he'd been pondering and pulled his laptop out of his bag. Layla came back down with a couple of coloring books and a big box of crayons. She set them on the coffee table.

Lowell looked over his drawings. "Hey, you want to help me with something?"

"What?" She flipped through a coloring book to find a clean page.

"Well, I'm designing a website for this book about bunnies. I need to know what colors are best. If I gave you some drawings, could you pick the colors you like the most?"

"Okay!" Layla sat up straight.

Her face was so much like her father's that it was uncanny. There were traces of Jase in her smile, in the shape of her eyebrows, even in the way she bit her lip when she was thinking hard. The look on her face threw Lowell off his game temporarily. He took a deep breath and refocused. "Okay, let me show you the drawings."

A while later, Lowell's assignment done, they got down to the serious business of coloring. Layla assigned Lowell a page with Dora the Explorer while she colored a page full of dinosaurs.

"Daddy took me to the museum in New York where they have dinosaurs," Layla said. "And all the dinosaurs were brown. But that's wrong. T. Rex is red."

"Not blue?" Lowell asked.

Layla pursed her lips and raised her eyebrows. "Dinosaurs aren't blue."

"Oh."

"But I think stegosaurus is purple."

"Of course," Lowell said.

They colored in silence for a while. Wanting to keep their rapport going, he asked, "How's T-ball camp going?"

"Good. Our last game is next Friday. It's against Camp Whitlock."

"Cool. Is your team any good?"

"We're the best, duh."

They continued to chat about T-ball, with Lowell struggling to apply his thin knowledge of the sport, and Layla humoring him when he asked a stupid question. When coloring was done, he found some blank paper in his bag and drew her some cartoony dinosaurs, including a T. Rex with a big bow on her head. Layla told him he was crazy, but then they both laughed at the drawings, and Layla colored them in.

* * *

Jase felt weary when he left the office, wondering how much longer he could really do this job. Could he could really deal with crises like this with increasing frequency, was he even willing to sacrifice a night with Layla for the bullshit his supervisor was presently putting him through?

He tried to put everything out of his mind as he drove home. When he opened his front door, he saw Lowell and Layla passed out in front of the TV. Lowell sat up, his head resting on the back of the couch, his mouth agape. Layla curled up next to him, her head on his shoulder, a fistful of his T-shirt in her hand. Seeing them curled up together made Jase's chest hurt.

He glanced back at the television and saw that one of the princess movies had been playing, but they must have fallen asleep before it ended, because the screen was showing the DVD menu. He switched off the TV, and the change in noise and lighting made Lowell stir. He put a protective arm around Layla but smiled when he realized the intruder was Jase.

Lowell's movements woke up Layla, who whined and then cuddled tighter against him.

Jase reached over and ruffled her hair. "Come on, princess, it's time for bed."

She said, "I'm not a princess."

"I was talking to Lowell."

Layla sat up and looked at Lowell. "He's not a princess."

"I'm a little bit of a princess," Lowell said.

Layla giggled.

Jase picked her up. He told Lowell to stay put, and he carried Layla upstairs. She curled into him and rested her head on his shoulder. He reflected sadly that he wouldn't be able to do this much longer, that she would soon be too heavy to carry. He laid her down on her bed. He was impressed that, though they'd fallen asleep downstairs, Lowell had had the presence of mind to put her in pajamas.

"Did you brush your teeth?"

"Yes, Daddy. Lowell made me."

"Good." He smoothed her hair away from her face. "Did you have a good time?"

She yawned. "Yeah, it was great. I helped Lowell with his work, and we made dinosaurs, and then we watched *Sleeping Beauty.*"

"That's good."

"Mmm." Layla was already on her way back to sleep. Jase kissed her forehead and pulled up her covers, then turned out the light and went back downstairs.

Lowell had stretched himself along the length of the couch and fallen back to sleep. Jase sat on the edge and patted Lowell's butt. "Come on, princess, wake up."

Lowell eased awake and smiled. "I've got a tiara and everything."

"I'll bet."

"A very cute boy gave it to me at Pride last year, on account of I'm so beautiful."

"You *are* beautiful," Jase said.

Lowell grinned. He grabbed the collar of Jase's shirt and pulled him down for a kiss. It was sweet and sleepy.

"Seriously, how did things go? I'm sorry you had to sit through the princess movie."

"Are you kidding? *Sleeping Beauty* is one of my favorites. It's a beautiful piece of animation. Plus, when I was a kid it was my mom's favorite too. She had it on VHS and used to watch it all the time. I decided even then that it was smart to keep it to myself that I identified with Aurora. I wanted Prince Phillip to come rescue me with a kiss too." Lowell's smile turned mischievous. "Of course, the prince who came to wake me up tonight was much more handsome."

Jase blushed. "That's really hokey," he said, though he was charmed.

"I know. Anyway, it was fine. I let her help me with a work project. I'm designing a website for this series of books starring a little white bunny who solves garden mysteries. I was trying to work out if the main part of the site should be blue or purple. Layla convinced me purple was the way to go."

Jase looked at the coffee table. "You didn't have to let her help you," he said, picking up the drawings there. There was a series of pages with goofy cartoon dinosaurs drawn on them. "Did you draw these?"

"Yeah. Layla did the color work, though."

"These are really great."

"They're just silly drawings. Although—fair warning—Layla wanted to hang them up. I told her she'd have to ask you."

"I'll put them on the fridge."

Lowell stretched his long body, throwing his arms over his head and sticking his legs out toward the coffee table. "I should probably go home before I fall back to sleep on your couch."

Jase stood to make room for Lowell to get up. "Seriously, thank you for doing this. I really appreciate it."

"Not a problem." Lowell yawned and ran his fingers through his hair in an unsuccessful attempt to flatten it. He stood and looked at Jase. "You look beat."

Beat is a good word, Jase thought. He bit his lip and nodded.

"You okay?" Lowell stepped forward and pulled Jase into his arms.

Jase let himself be held and dropped his head forward to rest it on Lowell's shoulder. "I'm fine. Exhausted, but I'll be all right in the morning—when I have to get up to do this all over again."

Lowell didn't say anything, just held him and rubbed his back. It felt so good to be held, so comforting, like coming home. He suddenly had a flash of many nights, coming home from work to find Lowell and Layla together in his living room, as if that were a perfectly natural state of affairs. He dismissed the image quickly and then eased himself out of Lowell's hug.

"Thanks," Jase said.

"*De nada.*" Lowell picked up his bag and slung it over his shoulder. "Sleep well, Prince Charming. I'll see you soon, I'm sure."

"Yeah." Jase smiled. "Good night."

He stood at his front doorway and watched Lowell disappear into his house.

Chapter Ten

Jase sat with Layla in Schuster's and watched her try to squash down her hamburger so that it was flat enough to shove into her mouth. He ate a french fry and felt relatively content.

"Hey, Layla!" shouted a little girl's voice.

Jase turned and saw Layla's friend, Susie, and her mother, Megan. Jase stood to greet them and got a quick hug from Megan for his trouble. The girls started chattering away.

"How are you?" Jase asked Megan.

"We're doing okay. You?"

"Just fine."

"Daddy, can I go sit with Susie?" Layla asked.

Jase looked at Megan for confirmation. She nodded. "Sure, kiddo." He considered sitting with them also. He liked Susie's parents, but he and Megan rarely had much to talk about. On the other hand, Neal was working the bar. "I'm going to go sit at the bar and talk to Uncle Neal. Let me know when you're ready to go."

"Okay!" Layla took her plate. The girls giggled and sat at an empty table with Megan.

Jase walked up to the bar and slid onto a stool. Neal smiled and poured him a soda. They chatted about the previous night's Yankees game. Jase heard the front door open and whoever came in caught Neal's attention. Jase turned to see who it was. Karen sauntered in, and given the slight sway in her step, she was already drunk.

"Shit," Jase said under his breath.

"Fan-fucking-tastic," said Neal. "I'll throw her out, if you want."

"No, that's okay. Let's see if she causes a problem first."

Karen strutted over to the bar. She shot Jase a flirty smile before perching on the stool next to his. "Hey, hot stuff," she said.

"Uh." Jase frowned. "Hi, Karen. Layla's here, so try to keep the fact that you're hammered to yourself."

"I'm not drunk," she said. She put a hand on his arm. "Where is Layla?"

"Sitting with Susie and her mother. But don't go talk to her. I don't want her to see you like this."

"I'm not drunk." She ran a hand up Jase's arm. There had been a hundred nights like this when he and Karen had sat at this very bar together. He'd drink while he let her put the moves on him. Then they'd go home and have perfunctory sex. Her touch seemed innocent now, but he recognized it for what it was.

He picked up her hand and placed it on the bar. "We're not married anymore."

"That doesn't mean we can't have sex."

"Actually, it does," Jase said. He scooted the stool over, hoping to put some distance between them. He eyed Neal, who had gone to the other side of the bar to help another customer. "I'm not doing this. First of all, Layla is right over there. Second, we're divorced. It's not appropriate." Not to mention that he *really* did not want to have sex with Karen.

When Jase looked at her, she was pouting. Her eyes were bloodshot. She was not a bad-looking woman, quite the contrary; Jase thought her beautiful, with her dark hair and pale skin. When their marriage started to fall apart, and Karen had finally confronted him, she'd asked if she turned him gay. He'd quickly disabused her of that, had tried to convince her that there was nothing wrong with her, but he wondered if the damage wasn't done. She'd tried, quite aggressively, to win him back after that, which, if anything, only pushed him away more.

He wondered if that was what she was doing now. She had on a shirt that showed off a tremendous amount of cleavage.

"You know," she said. "We could drop Layla off at my parents' place, then we could—"

"No."

Karen recoiled like he'd spit on her. She backed off and looked down at the bar for a moment. She was quiet for so long that he thought maybe she'd give up and leave. Then she lunged and kissed him.

He didn't see it coming, and he was too surprised to turn away at first. He'd spent a fair amount of time kissing Lowell recently, and he'd grown accustomed to the way Lowell's stubbly face felt against his own, to how Lowell smelled.

Despite the fact that he'd kissed Karen thousands of times when they'd been married, this kiss felt completely foreign. Once he was able, he pulled away. "Stop it. Come on, Karen, knock it off."

Her eyebrows came together, and her face became red. "Well, fuck," she said, throwing up her hands. "Maybe you really are gay!"

Her voice was drunk-loud, and Jase saw a few heads turn. He shushed her and said her name.

She leaned an elbow on the bar and faced him. "I could imagine, you know, you leaving me for someone. It's almost funny. I could tell my friends, 'Oh, you know, Jason left me for a man,' and we'd giggle. Or if you left me for another woman, I could get mad about that. But there are few things more embarrassing that being left just because you think you're gay."

"I'm sorry."

"I could have stayed, you know. I could have gone on forever. I was pissed the day I filed for divorce, but I might have gotten over it, and we could have made something work. Maybe then I wouldn't be living on my friends' couches. Maybe I'd have found a job, or maybe I wouldn't have needed one. I could stay home to take care of Layla."

Jase just shook his head, unable to speak. After all the time he'd spent with Lowell lately, learning what his life could be like, the idea of getting back together with Karen turned his stomach.

She crossed her arms over her chest. "No, instead, you're a fag."

"Karen, shut up."

"What? It's okay to tell me that to make our marriage end, but you don't want anyone else to know? Or was that a lie too?"

"It wasn't a lie," Jase whispered.

"But it is a secret. So, I could make a threat. Like, give me some money, or I'll tell everyone in this bar that you're gay."

"You wouldn't."

"Try me."

Neal slid a hand between them then. He turned to Karen. "I'm going to call you a cab," he said.

Then Layla came tearing across the restaurant. "Mommy!"

Karen got off the stool and knelt on the floor. She hugged Layla.

"What are you doing here?" Layla asked.

"I just came by, because..." She looked up at Jase. He wondered how she'd even known he was here, but figured it was just a coincidence. She shook her head. "I have to go now," she said.

Neal came around the bar and escorted Karen outside.

* * *

Lowell marveled at the density of the muscles in Jase's upper back, how knotted and tense his shoulders were. He straddled Jase's bare ass and gently kneaded those muscles, trying to do his part to ease some stress. He seemed to be having success with that, as Jase took a deep breath and finally started to relax, the tension in his back easing. Jase closed his eyes. He seemed to be falling asleep as Lowell moved lower, rubbing the muscles all along his back, running fingers over warm, smooth skin.

Lowell loved looking at Jase's back. He liked the straight line of it, the muscular width of Jase's shoulders, the way the muscles curved. He loved touching it too, loved getting his hands on all that skin and muscle. He thought Jase's body a thing of beauty, strong and masculine without being too big or overwhelming.

He was falling for the man that inhabited that body too. Lowell leaned down to kiss Jase's shoulder and got a sleepy sigh in response. So much of this adult Jase was not what Lowell would have expected, and that was all to the good as it forced Lowell to get to know the man he'd become, not to dwell on the boy he'd been.

And what a man he was, sweet and sensitive, smart and strong, caring and confused, and a little belligerent at times. And so alluring. Lowell's cock hardened as he moved lower on Jase's body, as he got his hands on more of that skin.

He backed up as he massaged the skin along the sides of Jase's hips and was greeted with the sight of the twin cheeks of Jase's very lovely tight, round butt. Lowell felt an overwhelming urge to shove his face between those two cheeks and just wallow there.

So he did. Lowell had put him to sleep, so Lowell decided he'd also wake him back up. When he ran his tongue along Jase's opening, Jase yelped.

He grabbed Jase's ass in both hands, and he leaned in and tasted. Jase whimpered as he pressed his tongue forward. He especially loved how Jase smelled, like something pleasant and musky. He inhaled deeply as he licked, the scent powerfully arousing. Feeling adventurous, he moved away slightly and nipped at one of those perfect cheeks. He got another yelp in response.

Jase shimmied his hips a little and got up on his hands and knees. Lowell smiled and ran his hands over the round mounds of Jase's ass. Then he pressed his face between the cheeks again, the scent driving him half mad. He licked and nibbled, and the smell and taste of Jase seemed to send electric currents through his body, straight toward his dick. He groaned as he felt Jase push at him. He was delighted when he heard Jase moan back.

Lowell moved away again and pressed Jase's hips back into the mattress. Jase grunted, but he persisted, sliding his own fingers into his mouth to wet them before he slid them between Jase's ass cheeks and circled around Jase's entrance. Jase hissed. Lowell looked at his face, turned sideways against the pillow, and saw he was lost, his eyes closed tightly, his hands twisted in the pillowcase. Lowell pressed a finger inside slowly and took the time to savor the tight warmth. He kissed the small of Jase's back, then trailed kisses over Jase's spectacular ass as he added a second finger.

Jase tensed up, so he moved his free hand to Jase's back and resumed massaging the muscles. "Relax, baby, relax," he whispered against the skin of Jase's hip. Jase sighed and took a deep breath, and like that, his body seemed to give way.

Lowell stretched him, prepared him, and soon had him moaning again.

"God, I want you," Jase said.

With some reluctance, Lowell moved away so that he could get a condom and the lube from the nightstand. He patted Jase's ass affectionately. Simply touching that smooth flesh spiked his arousal. He wanted this too, turned on beyond anything he could remember. He tore off the condom wrapper and tossed it on the floor. He rolled the condom on, then poured a generous amount of lube on his fingers.

His cock ached to be touched, and he wanted to be inside Jase's amazing body more than anything, but he made himself wait, attending to Jase, sliding his fingers inside Jase's entrance again. Jase moaned, and his hips jumped off the bed.

Lowell wanted to do this for Jase. He wanted his own pleasure too, but he wanted this to be good for Jase more. He nibbled and sucked on the skin of Jase's lower back as he slid a third lubed-up finger inside; all while Jase bucked against the mattress. When Lowell heard him panting and knew Jase was feeling just as frantic as he was starting to feel, he withdrew his fingers.

Jase whimpered again, a sound Lowell loved. He wanted to fill that emptiness in Jase, wanted to give in to that longing, wanted to see and try and do everything with this man. But most of all, he wanted to be inside Jase. He stroked his own cock with his lubed-up hands, and then he positioned himself behind Jase. His cock seemed to strain toward Jase's ass, seemed to know the way, seemed to belong nestled between Jase's ass cheeks. Lowell grasped Jase's hips in his hands and pushed forward, the head of his cock feeling the resistance of muscle. Then Jase said, "Oh God, Lowell, I need you," and Lowell moved forward, burying himself.

Jase was tight, his body seeming to close in around Lowell's cock, squeezing and stroking it as he slid out. Few things were more exquisite than this; few things would ever feel as good. Sweat broke out all over his body as he tried to restrain himself, tried to keep from pushing too hard or going too fast or doing anything that would hurt Jase, but this was too amazing. Lowell quickly felt himself losing his grip.

Jase moaned again and pushed back at Lowell, which spurred him to move faster. He wanted to savor, but he couldn't. He wanted that sweet release. He pumped in and out, seeking it but not ready to give in quite yet.

Then Jase cried out and grabbed at the pillow near his head and muttered, "Shit, I'm coming," while his hips bucked against Lowell's. Jase's body vibrated around Lowell's cock, and Lowell had to give in. Jase's body was hot and slick against his, around his, and every movement sent little electric pulses through his body, under his skin. He thought he might fly to pieces. And then there it was, and everything overwhelmed him. He shouted as he found release and slammed his hips against Jase's ass as he came. Then, spent, he collapsed on top of Jase.

Jase sighed happily, so Lowell was content to stay where he was until it started to get uncomfortable, until the sweat started to dry, and his skin got itchy. He slid out and rolled onto his back.

Jase reached over and hooked a hand behind Lowell's head and pulled him in for a kiss. Lowell thought maybe Jase didn't need to see, that his lips just found their way to Lowell's like they belonged there. They kissed for a long time, opening their mouths and exploring with tongues. Jase's lips were smooth and hot, and Lowell felt things stirring again, but more than that, he felt drawn into Jase. He was content to just lie in Jase's arms, kissing him, which was a sure sign that he was falling hard.

Finally, Jase backed away and opened his eyes. "Sex with you blows my mind," he said.

Lowell reached over and slid a hand over Jase's ass. "Likewise," he said. "Blows some other things too."

Jase laughed. He settled into the pillow. "I could fall asleep right here."

"So sleep."

Jase shifted his body slightly so he could look at his watch. "I have to pick Layla up in an hour."

"Ah, parental responsibilities."

Jase frowned. "Don't mock me."

"I'm not, I just… It's a tricky thing to get used to."

Jase yawned and scratched his head. "We had most of the weekend together."

"True." Lowell put his hand on Jase's back. "It's not like I don't see a lot of your ass."

"You like my ass."

Lowell smiled. "Very much."

Jase laughed and kissed him again before hoisting himself out of bed. Lowell admired his naked body as he left the room to go to the bathroom. He lay back on the bed and felt pretty lucky.

* * *

It was late on Sunday when the phone rang. Jase grabbed it, hoping it was Lowell, but when he answered the first thing he heard was, "How could you let that man babysit?"

Jase opted to play dumb. "Who, Lowell?"

"Yes, *Lowell.* I didn't want to say anything in front of Layla, but when she was here this weekend, she went on and on about Lowell and how you left him alone in your house with her!"

Jase rubbed his eyes. "I had to go into the office. Lowell is my friend, and I trust him."

"Well, I don't."

"You've never made me run babysitters by you before."

"You could have called me. I would have taken her if you had an emergency."

"Karen, come on. That doesn't make sense anyway. I'm not going to drive half an hour to drop her off when Lowell, who lives next door, is available to watch her in her home. It's better that she sleeps in her own bed on a school night. Or a camp night, I guess. Besides, you've never had a problem with me hiring babysitters before. This is no different."

"It's completely different. I don't like this guy."

A headache bloomed at the base of his skull. "You don't *know* this guy. You've never met him. Layla was fine. She had a great time."

"This guy is your friend."

"Yes, he's my friend. Shouldn't that be reason enough to trust him? To trust my judgment?" Jase sat up. He didn't miss the implication in the word "friend," but he wasn't sure if it was worth addressing.

"I don't know if your judgment is sound in this case. Especially if you're thinking with your dick."

He sighed. "You're upset because Lowell is gay. That's all this is about, right?" Jase knew better, of course. If only this were about Karen's homophobia. There was so much more going on here, and Jase knew also that he'd probably never be able to win this argument with logic or reason.

"Are you fucking him?"

Because that was really the issue here, wasn't it? Jase alone was no threat to Karen, even if he were attracted to men. But Jase in a relationship with someone else was.

Jase let her words hang in the air longer than he should have, but he made a good show of huffing to seem insulted. "I'm going to hang up the phone now."

"Look, I don't care if he's gay, but you need to be careful about bringing him around Layla."

Jase didn't know what to make of that. "What's the problem here? If it's not a problem that he's gay, why can't I let him be around Layla?"

"Because you promised…"

"Karen, we are not married. We have not been married for almost two years. You have no say in who I spend my time with."

"No, but I'm Layla's mother, and I do have a say in who spends time with her. I do not want Lowell around her anymore."

Jase had been expecting this fight, and it still made him feel tired and hurt. "He lives next door. That's not possible."

"Find a way to make it possible."

"Or what?" He realized he was being childish.

"I want to trust you, Jason, I do, but a mother has to protect her child."

"What does that even mean?"

"It means we had an agreement, but everything has changed now, which means I might have to take action."

"What the hell are you talking about? Nothing has changed! It's the same arrangement we've always had. You can't get this worked up over the fact that I've made friends with my neighbor." At her scoff, he added, "You're being completely unreasonable." He realized as he finished speaking that she'd hung up.

He sat back on the couch and stared at the phone. Karen didn't have any recourse the way Jase saw it, but he wondered if she had it in her to do something crazy. He didn't think so, and besides, what was there to even react to? She didn't know what was really going on with Lowell.

And what was going on with Lowell? Jase wasn't sure he knew, either. They'd been having really good sex. No, "really good" was too mild a description for it, but Jase didn't have the vocabulary to describe what Lowell did to him, how Lowell made him feel. Just that afternoon, they'd had sex until it felt like his brain had melted.

But was it more than that? He certainly liked Lowell— liked him a hell of a lot—but he knew also that sex on the sly was probably as far as it would ever go, as far as it *could* ever go. There was no way Jase could parade around town with Lowell on his arm like a boyfriend. And it wasn't like Jase could just invite Lowell over any time. He had promised that he wouldn't expose Layla to the people he dated, and he still intended to keep that promise.

Because he and Lowell weren't really *dating*. Sure, they went out to eat occasionally and hung out together when they both had time free, Jase told himself, but that wasn't the same as dating.

No, they were just friends. Friends who sometimes had ridiculous, amazing, brain-dribbling-out-of-your-ears sex.

Layla wandered into the living room and sat on the couch. "Are the Yankees playing?" she asked.

Jase looked at the TV. There was indeed a Yankees game on. He'd long since stopped paying attention. He turned up the volume. "Yeah. Baltimore."

"Oh good."

She crawled over and leaned against Jase, so he put an arm around her and let her snuggle against him. He sighed and tried to put things in perspective. This is what's important, he thought. But if this was all there was, why did he feel so sad about it?

Chapter Eleven

Lowell gave his mother a tour of the house, apologizing for the lack of furniture. She seemed charmed by the place, and more to the point, she was having a pretty lucid day. "The Midlands lived on this block," she said.

"Yes. Jason still lives next door."

"You boys were thick as thieves. You spent all of your time together. Josie Midland was such a nice woman. You remember?"

"Yeah, Mom, I remember. Do you want some tea or something?"

"Yes, tea would be nice."

He led her into the kitchen and put on a pot of water to boil.

"I'm impressed," his mother said, sitting at the kitchen table.

"This is all a far cry from the place in Manhattan. I feel like a real adult now." He fished through the cabinets for the box of herbal tea he knew his mother liked. He still drank it for comfort sometimes; it reminded him of the brief moments of calm in his childhood, the moments when his father had left the house in search of booze, the aftermath of some argument, when there was a reprieve between incidents.

"It's still a bit empty here," she said. "I've got more stuff in the house than I know what to do with. If there's anything you want…"

"I'm all right. I think I'd rather buy my own things."

"I never use the dining room table anymore. Or you could take the extra chairs from the basement."

Lowell had a brief flash of one of those chairs, upholstered in the same faded blue fabric that covered the Old Man's favorite chair and knew he wouldn't be able to look at any of them without seeing his father. "Thanks, Mom, but I've got some new chairs all picked out. They're from the same store I got the couch, so they'll match well."

He was saved from having to explain why he hated her furniture by the doorbell ringing.

"Are you expecting company?"

"No. It's probably someone trying to sell me something."

When he opened the door, Jase stood there, looking a little pensive.

"Hi," Lowell said.

"Hi. Um. Can I talk to you for a moment?"

Lowell motioned him inside. He closed the door behind Jase and watched him walk into the living room before he said, "My mother is here."

"Oh."

"Is something wrong?"

Jase rubbed his forehead. "No, not really. I mean, Karen and I had an argument about something completely stupid, but you know."

"Is that what you wanted to talk about?"

"Nah, I just…" Jase looked away, but there was a wistful smile on his face. "I guess I just wanted to see you."

Lowell grinned. He moved to close the space between him and Jase. There was a noise behind him, and his mother came out of the kitchen. "Lowell, who's at the door?"

"Mom, you remember Jason."

"Jason Midland," she said. "It's nice to see you all grown-up. How are you?"

"I'm all right." He took a step back, seeming to notice how close he was standing to Lowell.

"I left your tea on the counter, Lowell," she said. "Do you want something, Jason?"

"No, I'm fine. I just dropped by to say hello."

"You should have some tea with us. There's enough hot water for another cup."

Jase raised his eyebrows. "You're drinking hot tea in this weather? Have you noticed it's August?"

Lowell laughed. "Oh Jase. Let me introduce you to the great wonder that is afternoon tea. It will make all your troubles go away, at least for the next hour or so. I think I even have a box of shortbread cookies in the cabinet. Eh? What do you say?"

Jase shot Lowell's mother a wary look, but he nodded. "Sure, why not."

They all went back into the kitchen and sat around the table. Lowell got up and made Jase a cup of tea while Jase and his mother made small talk. She said, "I heard you have a daughter."

"Yes. Her name is Layla. She's six. She's at a friend's house for a sleepover."

Lowell could tell his mother was curious, but she sipped her tea instead of asking more questions. He placed a mug in front of Jase.

Jase blew at his tea. "So explain this afternoon tea thing to me."

Lowell smiled. He glanced at his mother, who smiled back. "Well, the first rule of afternoon tea is that you enjoy it. To take an hour not to think about your problems. You think you can do that?"

"I will try."

* * *

Jase walked into Schuster's and sat at the bar. He had only one objective. He pointed to the space in front of him and said, "Vodka."

Neal raised an eyebrow but put a shot glass in front of him and filled it with vodka. "Any special occasion?"

Jase bit his lip and looked at the bar. When he looked up again, he crossed his arms and said, "The person I am sleeping with did something really sweet for me this afternoon."

Neal put the bottle back on the shelf. "I didn't know you were sleeping with anybody. And this person did something sweet for you? That sounds like a real tragedy."

"Ha, ha." Jase uncrossed his arms and looked at the shot, appreciating how it burned all the way through his chest. He wasn't sure how to explain the problem to Neal. "I can't get involved. This was supposed to be just a sex thing. If it goes beyond that..."

Neal narrowed his eyes at Jase. "Why can't you get involved?"

"Because of Layla. Because I'm a father. I have other responsibilities. Because I promised Karen." Jase did the shot and slammed the glass back on the bar. He pointed to it.

Neal sighed and picked up the bottle of vodka again. He poured the shot. "I don't follow. How does who you date affect Layla enough for Karen to care?"

Jase did the second shot. His blood hummed as the alcohol started to seep through his body. He put the glass back on the bar and stared at it for a moment. Surely Neal knew. Surely he understood. "Karen doesn't like this person and doesn't want them to be around Layla. Plus I promised her that I wouldn't expose Layla to the people I dated. And now Karen's making...vague threats? I don't know. I mean, I know there isn't really anything she can do. She gave up custody. But I should live up to my end of the bargain, but this person... I just don't know what to do."

"Uh-huh. Another?"

"Yes."

Neal poured. "Who is 'this person'? Do I know her?"

Jase blinked at the pronoun and looked up. Neal's eyebrows were raised, like he expected something of Jase. Jase just said, "No."

"Right. Well. Seems to me that you got divorced almost two years ago and thus have the right to date whoever the hell you want. Fuck Karen."

Jase nodded. "Normally I'd agree, but Karen... I don't know. What if she does something?"

"What could she do? No court in its right mind would give custody to her. And it's not like she even has a place to live, right? Isn't she staying with her parents? They're not going to let her do anything too crazy."

"Yeah, I don't know. Maybe I'm worrying about nothing. And my...friend, it's not like we're going to go parading around town holding hands anyway." He did the third shot. He pointed to the glass.

Neal held the bottle but didn't pour another. "Jase, come on. You're a good father. Karen can't do anything to you, least of all over something as meaningless as who you go out with. If you were getting remarried, we might be having a different conversation, but dating? What is she gonna do about it? She's picking a fight with you because she can, because she knows how to get to you. She's jealous, that's all. She's got her panties in a twist because you're dating again. Finally."

"Give me another shot, Neal."

Neal sighed and poured it. "I hope to hell you aren't driving."

Jase felt light-headed enough that he started to worry he'd blurt something he wasn't ready to say. He decided to let the fourth shot sit for a moment.

"So, you are dating again," Neal said.

Jase shrugged. "Well, I don't think you can really call it that. We've been out together, like, twice. Otherwise, we have sex when Layla's away. And that's the other thing. How is that fair to the other person? Hi, I'm Jason. I think you're sexy as hell. I want you all the fucking time. I'm pretty sure you feel the same way about me, but we can only see each other, like, twice a month. Instead of a weekend dad, I'm a weekend boyfriend." He gave up holding out and did the fourth shot.

"Uh-oh," Neal said.

"What?"

"You have real feelings for this person. That's why you're getting hammered. You really care about whoever this is, and it scares the shit out of you."

"Please. It's just sex. It's not that big a deal."

"Right."

Well, there it was. Neal was right, of course. Jase did care about Lowell. In the past, he'd always acceded to Karen's wishes because the path of least resistance was the easiest to follow, but this time, he found he didn't want to go down that path. He wanted Lowell.

"Dammit," he said, slamming the shot glass on the bar again. "Another."

Neal poured another shot.

* * *

Even after giving things a few hours to process, Lowell felt a little confused and not sure what to do. Jase had never gotten the opportunity to talk to him about whatever he'd wanted to talk about, which was something that nagged at the back of Lowell's mind. Still, he went about his day, working in the living room for the rest of the evening. He was surprised when the doorbell rang around nine.

He wasn't that surprised though to see a disheveled Jase on the other side of the door.

"Don't say anything," said Jase. He swayed a little on his feet.

"Are you drunk?"

"It's possible." He looked up toward the sky thoughtfully. "Very possible." He took a step forward and propelled himself toward Lowell.

Lowell caught him. He felt anger bubble up almost instantly. He'd never had a problem with other people drinking, but something about Jase's shaky movements conjured up a few bad memories. He just did not have the energy to deal with someone this drunk, but he didn't want to turn Jase away either. "I hope to hell you did not drive home from wherever you got blitzed."

"Neal drove me home." Jase leaned against Lowell and looked up.

Lowell looked outside to make sure no one was there watching, and then he pulled Jase in and shut the door. "I'm going to put you to bed. We can talk about this in the morning."

"Are you going to bed with me?" Jase asked.

"No, not when you're out of it."

It took some work, but Lowell managed to get Jase to walk up the stairs and into the bedroom. Jase flopped on the bed. He rolled onto his side and looked up at Lowell. "I've got a hard-on like you wouldn't believe. Let's fuck."

"Nope. You're going to sleep this off."

"Karen's mad because I won't let her fuck me anymore." Jase giggled, then said, "No, I mean, because I won't fuck her. Duh, she doesn't have a dick, or else we wouldn't have this problem." He giggled again.

Lowell rolled his eyes and stood over Jase. "You want some coffee or something?"

"No. You have any beer?"

"You are not drinking anymore."

"I went to Schuster's after I left here this afternoon."

"Were you there all this time? No wonder you're hammered."

Jase patted the bed, but Lowell remained standing. Jase pouted and said, "Karen thinks you're going to molest Layla. I told her that you're not a pedophile. But, really, I think she's worried you'll molest me. I like when you molest me."

"Jase…"

"I think Neal is fucking some guy in town. See, everyone has secrets!"

"I'm going to get you some water. Don't go anywhere."

"Come back naked!" Jase shouted before dissolving into more giggles.

When Lowell got back to his room, Jase had fallen asleep. Lowell's disappointment was almost a palpable thing, but he knew this wasn't about him. He pulled the covers over Jase and turned off the lights.

* * *

When Jase woke up, the first thing he was aware of was the marching band stomping across his head. Before he opened his eyes, he tried to piece together the previous night. He'd gone to Schuster's, he knew that much. He had felt defeated and humiliated. He'd been working his way toward a really good drunk when Neal had put the brakes on it and driven him home.

Something else was wrong too. His bed felt different, and he was still wearing the clothes he'd had on the night before. He'd wanted to see Lowell when he got home, but he hadn't really gone over to his house, had he? There were Lowell's black sheets covering the mattress, and Lowell himself propped up on one elbow and looking at him.

Jase groaned. "God, I'm sorry."

"It's okay. How do you feel?"

"Like I've got an ax buried in my skull."

"Sit up," Lowell said.

Jase did so reluctantly. He was rewarded with aspirin and a glass of water. He swallowed it all and then handed the glass back to Lowell, who put it on the nightstand. "Did I say anything embarrassing last night?"

"Not really. There was something in there about you wanting me to molest you, which I didn't because you were drunker than I've seen anybody in a long time."

Jase remembered Old Man Fisher. He leaned back against the wall. "I'm an asshole. You must hate me."

"I won't lie and tell you I approve of you drinking that much, and I was pretty mad. Why did you get drunk? Was it about whatever you wanted to talk to me about yesterday?

"No. Well, yes," Jase said, massaging his temples with the tips of his fingers. He closed his eyes. The darkness helped. "Karen's giving me shit over my relationship with you. Or what she thinks my relationship with you is like. She says she doesn't want you around Layla, but really she doesn't want me to be happy, which I guess I understand."

"Don't apologize for her." Lowell slowly reached over and smoothed some of Jase's hair out of his face. "You have a right to your own life."

"Thank you for not throwing me out last night. I am really, truly sorry."

Lowell nodded, then leaned over and kissed him. Jase meant to protest stridently but instead found himself putting his arms around Lowell.

"I know you don't believe this," Lowell said, "but you deserve happiness."

Jase couldn't say anything. Instead, he pressed his face into Lowell's neck and held on tight.

Chapter Twelve

Jase lay awake in Lowell's bed, memorizing his back as he slept turned away. He had a mole on his left shoulder, and there were several long scars that marred the otherwise smooth skin. Jase wondered about those. Wanting to be close, he reached over and ran a hand up the side of Lowell's torso. He spooned up behind Lowell, pressing his nose into the back of Lowell's neck and inhaling. He was surprised to feel Lowell's hand move over his arm. "You awake?" Lowell asked.

"Yeah, I was having trouble sleeping."

"Mmhmm."

"Were you awake?"

"Kind of."

"I'm sorry. I didn't mean to wake you."

"I really don't mind."

Lowell took a deep breath, and his chest expanded against Jase. It was interesting, he thought, to share a bed with this man, especially after all those years with Karen. Karen was a petite woman. Lowell was thin but substantial, tall with wiry muscles, and more than that, Lowell had a presence that sometimes felt like it filled a room. Jase felt dwarfed by it on occasion, which was both intimidating and a relief. With Lowell, Jase didn't have to pretend. He didn't have to worry. Everything felt like it might be all right.

"Jase, are you okay?"

Jase closed his eyes. "Yeah."

Lowell shifted so that Jase could rest his head on Lowell's shoulder. Lowell kissed Jase's forehead. "No, really."

"I'm okay," Jase said. "I feel okay when I'm with you." He propped himself up on his elbow so that he could look down on Lowell's face. It was so handsome, even when Lowell's hair was disheveled, even when Lowell's eyes were sleepy. "I feel bad about waking you up."

"Really, it's fine," Lowell said. "My mind was wandering into some not so good places, so I'm grateful for the distraction."

Jase found that surprising. "What places?"

Lowell put a hand on Jase's back. "I don't..."

"Come on," Jase said. "You can tell me."

Lowell hesitated, but then said, "I'm worried about my mother. She's not well. I mean, leaving her keys in the refrigerator, that kind of not well. I don't think it's simple forgetfulness. I scheduled a doctor's appointment for next week. I hope it's just temporary, that she's still reeling from the Old Man's death, but it might be more serious. I don't know what I will do if it is." Sensing Lowell had more to say, Jase didn't speak. After a long pause, Lowell said, "I feel like such an impostor. I've been away for a long time, and I drop back in now only to find out something is probably really wrong. We've hardly spoken for years, but now it's up to me to take care of her. It's surreal."

"Why did you stay away for so long?"

Lowell blinked rapidly a few times, then looked at Jase. His eyes widened in surprise. "You really don't know?"

"Your father? I heard rumors, but I never knew for sure."

Lowell closed his eyes and nodded.

"Those scars on your back?"

"From the Old Man's belt."

"Lowell."

Lowell opened his eyes. "He was an alcoholic. No, he was more than that. Old Man Fisher was the fucking town drunk, and everyone knew it. He was functional, though, or functional enough to take out his aggressions on me and Mom." Lowell's voice broke. He swallowed and said, "I was afraid to go home a lot of the time, not sure what would set him off."

"I wish I had known at the time."

"What could you have done? We were kids. My mom wasn't enough to stop him. She'd try. She'd get in his face and tell him I was just a boy, and then he'd hit her."

"Lowell."

"I wasn't sad when he died. Mom called me to tell me, and I didn't feel anything. I hadn't spoken to him—I mean had a real conversation with him—in almost twenty years. I turned eighteen and blew out of Greenbriar, and I did not look back. My father hated me, hated who I was, and so did most of this town, and I thought, 'Fuck him, fuck the whole town,' and I went, and I lived my life. My old man just got drunker until he drank himself to death, and I felt nothing when he died." He frowned and looked at Jase. "Is that wrong?"

Jase touched Lowell's face. He felt sympathy, and guilt for not seeing what was going on all those years ago, and awe that Lowell had come through it such a strong man. He felt guilt, also, for showing up drunk on Lowell's doorstep, could only imagine what Lowell must have felt when that happened. "I don't think it's wrong," he said. "And I'm an asshole for showing up here so drunk last week. You should have kicked me out."

"I find I have a hard time turning you away."

Jase rested his head on Lowell's shoulder again. He wanted to offer something to Lowell, but wasn't sure what he could do. All he knew was that Lowell had helped him immensely, and he wanted to return the favor. "If you need anything," he said. "I mean, if you want some help with your mother. I've got some connections at medical facilities in the region. I could get some information about..."

Lowell sighed. "No, thank you. I've got it."

"Are you sure? Because I could—"

"No, really, Jase. I don't need your help."

Jase wasn't sure what to do with that, but there was finality in Lowell's voice, so he decided to drop it. They lay together silently, and Jase felt mostly content.

After a while, Lowell asked, "What happened to your parents, if you don't mind my asking?"

Jase didn't like to think about his parents, "Mom died of breast cancer right after I married Karen. Dad followed not long after, some kind of congenital heart problem he'd had forever but never told anyone about. I think after Mom died, he stopped fighting it and just kind of let go."

"That's terrible."

Jase nodded. "It was hard to watch."

"To lose them both close together must have been hard."

"Yeah."

"And Karen helped you through it?"

"Some of it, yes. She was the only one willing to listen to me cry about it. Even Neal and Russ, who are supposed to be my closest friends, kind of backed off when Mom died, not because they're bad people, but I think they just didn't know what to say to me. Karen was really there for me, though. So you can see why it's hard for me to hate her."

"And she's the mother of your child and all that."

"That too."

Lowell ran a hand through Jase's hair. "I always liked your mother. If I had known she'd died, I would have come up for the funeral."

"No, you wouldn't have, but it's okay. She was a great woman. I still miss her a lot."

"I wish things with us had gone differently. For what it's worth, I would have listened."

"You should have told me about your father."

"Can you blame me for not telling you?"

"No." Jase wanted it all back to do over again. He wanted to help the boy Lowell had been, he wanted to get help from the man Lowell was now, and he wanted Lowell in his arms, in his bed, for as long as he could have him. He lifted his head and kissed Lowell, and he savored the sensation of their lips touching, of Lowell's scratchy face, of the way he tasted. Lowell put his arms around Jase and held him tightly.

Jase got hard, the proximity and the smell of Lowell more arousing than anything. Lowell put a hand on Jase's bare ass and squeezed. "I see what's going on here," he said.

"What?" Jase thrust his hips against Lowell's.

"You're parlaying an emotional conversation into sex. You figured you'd get me all vulnerable and then have your way with me."

"That's not what I'm doing," Jase said, though Lowell's erection was hard to ignore. He moved his hand between them and wrapped it around Lowell's cock.

Lowell hissed. "I know. I'm just teasing." His lips danced along the edge of Jase's jaw. He kissed Jase's neck and sucked on one spot gently. "You are so sexy," he murmured. "Like all my fantasies come to life. And you're here, and you're with me, and I want you all the time."

"Me too." Jase was so overwhelmed by the magic Lowell's mouth was making that he found it hard to think. "I want you, I mean."

Lowell kissed him and snaked his fingers through his hair, pulling a little. Jase groaned, liking that little bit of pain.

"You want me right now?" Lowell nibbled at Jase's ear.

"God, yes." Jase touched Lowell's chest, squeezed a nipple between his fingers. "I love when you fuck me."

"Say that again," Lowell said, breathless now, hard and panting and putty under Jase's hands. The more Lowell fell apart, the hotter and harder Jase became.

"I love when you fuck me."

Lowell moaned and kissed Jase hard. "I'm happy to comply, then. And I want you to be happy. Are you happy now, Jase?"

"I'm happy when I'm with you," Jase said, which felt true.

"I want to make you happy." Then he lowered his voice. "I want to fuck you, and I want you to love it. I want you moaning and panting, and I want you to come with me inside you."

"Yes."

Lowell bit Jase's earlobe, which hurt in the best way, sending lightning bolts through Jase's body. Jase felt him smile against his cheek. Lowell shifted their bodies so that Jase was on his back, and Lowell hovered above. He moved away long enough to grab lube and a condom from the nightstand, but he never completely let go of Jase, one hand always touching him somewhere.

He handed Jase the condom and said, "Put this on me." Jase put his hand around Lowell's cock and stroked, feeling the smooth hardness under his fingers, reveling in that, knowing Lowell was hard for *him*. He wanted that hardness moving inside him, so he slowly rolled the condom on, squeezing and stroking as he did it. He loved the little growly sounds Lowell made in the back of his throat.

Lowell's fingers were soft like feathers as he touched exactly where Jase wanted to be touched. Jase pulled his knees up to his chest. Lowell moved down between his legs and licked him there. The sensation was still odd at first, wet and foreign, but it eased into pleasure as Lowell's tongue sought entrance. He had never been rimmed before he'd been with Lowell, but he'd liked it the last time Lowell did it. Lowell seemed to know exactly how to touch and lick to wake up his senses, to make his skin tingle. Jase moaned appreciatively.

Lowell moved and began sucking on Jase's balls while he slowly inserted one, then two fingers, stretching Jase. Jase was going out of his mind. Everything Lowell did made him jerk and move and strain toward Lowell's hand and fingers. He grew frantic wanting more, needing Lowell. Lowell's tongue moved from the base of Jase's cock to the tip as he inserted a third finger. There was a burst of intense pain that quickly subsided, the rough texture of Lowell's tongue on his sensitive skin making him quake, making him want more. Everything was wet and warm and made him writhe. He could have come right then, but he fought back the orgasm, grunting with the effort. He moaned out Lowell's name.

Lowell climbed back on top of him with a grin on his face. "Do you want me?"

"Yes, God yes." He wanted this. He *needed* this. Was there any answer but *yes?*

Lowell dipped his head and kissed Jase hard, first sucking on Jase's lower lip, then thrusting his tongue inside. Jase felt the tip of Lowell's cock seeking entrance, so he grabbed Lowell's ass to encourage him. Lowell moved with frustrating slowness, but it felt like the head of his cock hit every nerve ending as he pushed forward, and then he was fully inside.

Jase loved this feeling of being filled and complete. He held Lowell close, their chests pressing together, hearts pounding against each other as Lowell moved inside him, scraping against nerves and making Jase's very skin feel hot and alive. They kissed, and Jase felt something rise up his chest, a warm feeling, and all he could think about was that he loved being with this man.

He was broadsided by the orgasm, rocking against Lowell one moment, losing himself to the heat and the pleasure of their bodies sliding together, and then spurting between them the next. Lowell kissed him as he came, then held him while he continued to move. Jase touched Lowell everywhere he could, stroking his back, running his hands down Lowell's chest, pinching his nipples. Lowell's skin broke out in goose bumps, and sweat trickled down his face. Jase wanted Lowell to come, wanted him to feel everything Jase was feeling. Lowell's nipples tightened under Jase's fingers, and his body writhed. Lowell closed his eyes and picked up the pace, became frantic, then came on a long moan. He collapsed on top of Jase and kissed his face all over, repeating his name.

Lowell got up to take care of the condom. Jase rolled over onto his side and felt bereft suddenly, empty without Lowell, taken off guard by the intensity of his feelings. Tears stung his eyes, and he pressed his face into the pillow to hide them. He didn't want to feel this strongly, knew he shouldn't want this emotional connection with another man as badly as he did.

When Lowell came back, he sat on the bed for a long moment looking down at Jase. Then he scooted down next to him. "Are you okay?"

Without moving his head from the pillow, Jase said, "Yeah."

"Jase?"

It was clear Lowell wouldn't be convinced otherwise, so Jase shifted to look at him. Lowell immediately put a hand on Jase's face and touched a tear. The gesture was so sweet, and it only served to remind Jase that this was temporary, that it had to be. It would never last, never be the relationship it should have been. He only had this moment. The thought made him feel lost, empty, and his eyes stung again.

"God, Jase, what is it?"

"I…" He didn't know what to say. He couldn't find the words to express what he felt. "I didn't know. I didn't know it could be like that."

Lowell looked into his eyes, concern on his face. "Like what? Was it bad? Did I hurt you?"

"No," Jase put a hand on Lowell's side, willing Lowell to move closer. "No, it was really good. I'm sorry." He buried his face in the pillow. What he wanted to say was that he hadn't known sex could be that tender and affectionate and still that intense and wonderful.

"What are you apologizing for? Don't apologize. What did I do? How can I make it better?"

Jase put his arms around Lowell and hugged him close. He pressed his face against Lowell's shoulder and fought against the tears, but they continued to come anyway. He felt such relief in Lowell's arms. Lowell held him, and Jase knew he was baffled, but Jase couldn't figure out what to say. He took several breaths. "It was good. You're so good to me, and I wasn't expecting… It just felt really intense, and I don't know why I'm crying. I'm such a baby, I…"

Lowell laughed softly. "It's okay." He stroked Jase's back. "You need to cry, you cry all over me. It's different, isn't it, with someone you care about rather than just some one-night stand or a blowjob in a back room."

Jase tried to jerk away, but Lowell held him firm. Reluctantly, he said, "Yeah, it's different."

Lowell didn't say anything, just continued to lie there.

Jase knew that in a few hours, he'd have to leave this house, leave Lowell behind, and the prospect of that made him sad. Having to face work and Karen and everything that existed outside of the four walls of Lowell's bedroom made him feel sick to his stomach. He had this great thing now, but what would he do when he left Lowell's house? It didn't exist in the outside world. It couldn't exist.

He knew this was just a taste. He didn't know how it would ever work, this relationship with Lowell.

Something occurred to him suddenly. "How did you deal with your father? It must have felt like it would never end. Where did you find the strength to keep going?"

Lowell was quiet for a long moment. Eventually, he said, "Hope, I guess. And I knew it wasn't forever. I knew I'd turn eighteen and leave for college, and I'd never go back. You have to hope, Jase. Things can get better."

"I don't see how sometimes, I really don't."

"I know, but it's true. You'll figure something out."

Jase couldn't imagine a world where he didn't have to go to the office, where he could keep Layla happy, where he could be with the person he wanted to be with without a threat hanging over him. There was too much to balance.

But being with Lowell gave him a few moments of happiness. And for that, he was grateful.

* * *

That evening, Lowell found Jase's jacket on the couch. He went next door and rang the bell. Layla answered and grinned. "Hi, Lowell."

Jase appeared behind her. "What's up?"

"You left your jacket at my place," Lowell said, holding it up. "Figured you might want it back."

"Lowell," Layla said. "Can you watch *Dora* with me?"

"Honey, Lowell is busy. He might not have time to watch movies with you."

"I have a little time. If it's okay with you." He looked at Jase.

"It's okay. Come on in."

Lowell sat with Layla on the couch and watched an episode of *Dora the Explorer,* a show he was completely unfamiliar with except for Dora's appearances in Layla's coloring books. Layla narrated the show for him to make sure he understood what was going on. Jase bustled around the room, putting things away, but eventually sat down and watched the last ten minutes of the show.

"Okay, kiddo," he said when the show was over. "Time for bed."

"Aw, Daddy!"

"Now, Layla."

Very dramatically, she got up, then dragged herself over to the staircase, then plunked her foot on each step on the way upstairs.

Lowell stood. "I should go."

"You didn't have to sit through the whole show."

"It was fine. I find that I like doing things to make Layla happy."

Jase smiled. "Yeah, she has that effect on people."

"She's a great kid. I like her a lot."

"The feeling seems to be mutual." Jase stood too. Quietly, he added, "Thank you."

"Look, we never got a chance to really..." He frowned. He thought that after this morning, something had changed. They needed to do something, to say something, even if it were only a discussion about what they were doing together. "We should talk. Not now, obviously, but soon."

Jase rubbed his forehead. "Yeah. I owe you that."

"You don't owe me jack. Just, we should figure out what this thing is." At Jase's horrified expression, Lowell hastily added, "I don't want to push you into anything. Just saying."

"Yeah, I know."

He looked so sad, it caused a pang in Lowell's chest. He reached over and lifted Jase's chin so that they could look into each other's eyes. "Hey, now. Not the end of the world. Everything will be fine. I have no complaints. For the record."

Jase shook his head. Then he smiled. "I'm glad you moved in. I don't regret anything."

Lowell took a step closer. "Me neither. Will Layla come back downstairs?"

"No, she shouldn't. I'll go tuck her in after you leave."

Lowell nodded. He reached over and traced his finger along Jase's jaw, then leaned in and kissed him. Lowell intended it to be to be a sweet, quick good-bye kiss, but Jase leaned in and opened his mouth. Lowell got caught up in it, lost in the heat and the slick slide of Jase's lips against his own. It wasn't like kissing Jase was a hardship.

Jase backed off eventually and smiled before walking Lowell to the door.

* * *

After Lowell left, Jase found himself unable to stop smiling. He went up the stairs and found Layla sitting on the top step, clad in her pajamas, a confused expression on her face.

"Come on, kiddo, go get in bed." When she didn't move immediately, Jase asked, "What's up?"

"How come Mommy doesn't like Lowell?"

Jase coaxed her up and guided her toward her room. "She doesn't know Lowell."

"She says I shouldn't see him anymore."

Jase watched Layla climb into bed. "What do you think about that?"

"I asked her why, and she said Lowell is a bad man. But you don't think Lowell is a bad man."

"No. Lowell is a good man. I like him a lot." He walked over to the bed and held up the covers for her to scoot under.

"I know." Layla slid under her quilt. "Mommy said he does things that are bad, but she wouldn't tell me what they are."

Jase wondered if it was better to just explain. She was only six—almost seven, she'd be sure to remind him—but on the other hand, she was a smart, articulate six-year-old. Layla looked at him expectantly. Jase tried to formulate a good explanation. "You know what? Sometimes Mommy and I are going to like different people. But I really like Lowell, and I want you to like him too. Mommy doesn't know Lowell very well, so she doesn't understand. Okay?"

Layla's eyebrows pressed together. "Lowell is nice. I don't get it. Mommy says he's different."

"Remember when we talked about Uncle Neal? And how some boys love other boys? Lowell is like that too."

"What about you?"

He took a deep breath. "What about me?"

"Do you like other boys?"

Jase marveled at her perceptiveness. He didn't know how to answer the question, though. More, he didn't want his answer reported back to Karen. "I don't know."

"You said it's okay."

"It is. It's a complicated thing. A grown-up thing. And you shouldn't worry about it, okay?"

"I want Lowell to be my friend," she said.

"He just told me he wants to be your friend too."

She smiled. "I don't care what Mommy says, then. I will be friends with Lowell."

Jase loved that she was so defiant. He leaned over and kissed the top of her head. "Mommy is right about most things. You should still listen to her. But I think it's also good to judge people for yourself, to not always listen to what other people tell you."

"Okay," she said. "Can I see Lowell tomorrow?"

"We'll see."

Layla lay back on the pillow. "I love you, Daddy."

"I love you too, kiddo. Sweet dreams."

Chapter Thirteen

Jase sat at home the next Saturday when the bell rang. He opened the door and found Neal. Jase felt tired and wasn't really up for socializing, but he said, "Hey."

"Hey. The Yankees are playing the Red Sox. You have a better TV than I do. I brought beer." Neal held up a six-pack.

It had actually been a long-standing tradition, Jase and Neal watching Yankees/Red Sox matches together—Neal was an avowed Red Sox fan—but they'd only done it once so far this season. Jase felt sad suddenly, hating that he'd been neglecting the tradition, mostly missing hanging out with Neal on weekend afternoons. Nothing felt like it used to anymore. He nodded and opened the door wider. Neal walked in and plunked the six-pack on the coffee table.

"Is Layla home?" Neal asked as he made himself comfortable on the couch.

"No, Karen picked her up a little while ago. They went to the movies." Jase sat. He looked at Neal warily. "I'm sorry," he said quietly.

Neal raised his eyebrows. "What on earth are you apologizing for?"

"We haven't done this in a while, and I've been so busy with other things that I—" Then he abruptly shut his mouth.

He didn't want Neal to know what he'd been busy with, not until he'd worked through it in his own mind, though he suspected that Neal had already puzzled it out. He didn't really understand his own reluctance to just be honest with Neal, his friend, his *gay* friend, but he couldn't bring himself to say anything. He turned up the volume on the game.

Neal settled into the couch. The Red Sox were up by a run, but it was only the second inning. Neal slid a beer out of the six-pack and produced a bottle opener from his pocket. Jase was about to reach for a beer too when the doorbell rang.

Lowell was there this time. He grinned when Jase answered the door.

"What are you doing here?" Jase asked.

Lowell balked, his expression changing from happy to looking a little miffed. "Um, I came to say hello? It's Sunday afternoon, I happened to see Layla go off with Karen a little while ago, I thought we could…"

Jase ran a finger across his neck to try to make Lowell shut up. From the living room, Neal called, "Hi, Lowell!"

"Hey, Neal." Recognition dawned on Lowell's face. "I see," he said to Jase. He glanced back toward the driveway. "I suppose that explains the extraneous car. What are you guys up to?"

"Uh, just watching the ball game." Nausea crept through Jase's stomach, spreading quickly. His need to diffuse the situation was strong. Jase pushed Lowell out the door and pulled it closed behind him as he stepped onto the stoop. He looked around. They stood together on the stone walkway in front of the house. There didn't seem to be anyone out on the street. Lowell's brow furrowed when Jase looked at him.

"I can't do this right now," Jase said. "I think you should leave."

Now Lowell's eyes narrowed. "Oh I'm sorry. I didn't realize I needed an engraved invitation to stop by. What am I, after all? I'm not your neighbor or your friend or the *man who is fucking you.*"

"Shh!" Jase moved his hands as if he were pushing something down.

Lowell's eyebrows shot up. "Really?" he said. "Secret affair?"

"You had to have known that's the only way this could work. I can't just… I mean, it's not like we were ever going to be a real couple. We weren't ever going to parade down Main Street holding hands or anything. Greenbriar is not exactly a progressive town."

"Oh, don't give me that bullshit," Lowell said. "Believe me, I know all about how the people of Greenbriar treat gay people, and you know what? Maybe we wouldn't be able to walk around like a straight couple, but we have friends here who would understand, plenty of people who would accept us because they care about *us*, not that we're gay. Neal, for instance, who I assume you haven't told about us."

Jase shook his head. There was no way he could explain it to Lowell. "Karen—"

"Forget Karen. She's got nothing to do with this."

"I just… I can't, Lowell. You can't just stop by whenever. You have to be more careful. Because I'm not going to be your boyfriend. This thing between us…it's just sex."

Lowell's jaw loosened, and he took a step back as if Jase had just slapped him. "How can you say that?" His voice rose. "Is that what you really think? After everything that's happened?"

"That's all it can be."

Lowell stared at Jase for a long moment.

"Really good sex," Jase said.

Lowell took a long breath before he shrugged. "Fine. That's how you want to play this, that's how we'll play it. I'm just a good fuck. None of this meant anything to you. I'll see you later, Jase." He turned and started to walk toward his house.

And that wasn't right. Jase knew it. "Wait," he called.

Lowell turned.

"No, it's not… I mean, we *are* friends. Come in and watch the game with me and Neal."

Lowell shook his head. "What, so I can pretend that we're just buddies and everything is hunky dory? No, thank you."

"That's not what I…" Jase was at a loss.

"I'm just going to go home. I've got some shit to do."

Jase let him go. He watched Lowell retreat across the driveway and felt all the energy drain from his body. He stood on the walkway for several minutes after Lowell had gone back to his house, wondering if he'd just fucked everything up, but concluded that, even if he had, it was probably the right thing to do. Carrying on with a relationship—if that's even what it was—that was never going to go anywhere wasn't fair to anybody.

He went back into the house. Neal was still watching the game. He handed Jase a beer when Jase sat back on the couch.

"So. What was all that about?"

"Nothing."

"You didn't invite Lowell to watch the game?"

"He had something else to do."

"So he stopped by just to start an argument?" When Jase turned to look at him, Neal held up his hands. "I heard shouting, but I didn't hear anything either of you said."

"It's nothing."

"Uh-huh."

"Things with me and Lowell, they aren't.... I mean, he just stopped by to say hi, but..." Jase frowned. He wasn't sure what to do now. Kick Neal out, then run next door, apologize profusely? Let Lowell stew? Break it off for good? Become celibate? "I mean, it's not a big deal."

"Jase, shut up." Neal spat out the words with surprising force. "Just shut up. Stop lying to me. You don't have to. I won't judge you. I'm gay, remember? I know about you, so I think it's time we stop pretending."

"What are you talking about?" Panic kicked in. Jase's heart rate went up, and his insides churned. This was a conversation with Neal that was probably long overdue, but he didn't want any part of it. He wasn't ready to tell Neal the truth yet. He asked himself why, because he should have been able to talk to Neal about this, but he wasn't.

Because that made it real.

"You and Lowell," Neal said.

"Yeah? What?"

Neal sighed. "Okay. I have to spell it out. This 'person' you've been sleeping with. The one who inspired you to get so ridiculously drunk a couple of weeks ago. It's Lowell."

"How do you know that?"

Neal tapped his head. "Because I know you, and I've gotten to know Lowell pretty well. He comes into the bar during weekday afternoons to hang out and work sometimes. I'd say we've gotten to be pretty good friends in that time. Plus, you know, I have eyes."

Jase grunted, trying to sound dismissive, but that really worried him. If Neal had picked up on it…

"I don't think anyone else knows," Neal said quietly. "They wouldn't have been looking for it."

"Were you?"

Neal looked at his beer. "Yeah, since you mentioned you were seeing someone. It didn't escape my notice that you were careful about pronouns. And, I mean, come on. I've had thirty-four years to perfect my gaydar."

Jase sighed, feeling defeated. "How long have you known?"

"About you? A while, I don't know. Probably since before you married Karen."

"And you never said anything."

"It wasn't my place. We all have to do this on our own time. I do recall trying to talk you out of getting married."

"Yeah." Jase rubbed his forehead. "I know." He remembered Neal's words almost exactly. "*This is the biggest mistake you will ever make*" had certainly been part of that speech, and the words had echoed through his head often. At the time, he'd been angry and hadn't spoken to Neal for most of the week between the bachelor party and the wedding. If only he'd listened.

"You don't have to prove anything to me, Jase. We've been friends for a billion years. You were supportive of me when I came out. Why would you think I wouldn't be the same for you?"

"I don't know." Jase shook his head. "That's not why I didn't. I mean, that's not what this is about. I just couldn't tell you. I didn't want to. Because saying it out loud…"

"Made it true."

"Yeah."

"This is not the worst thing that ever happened to you." Neal finished off his beer and put the bottle back on the table. "I know you're worried and a little ashamed, but there's nothing to be ashamed of. Stop treating being gay like it's the same as getting cancer. You were born this way. You seem to have come around to the fact that you can't change it. I kind of thought that's what happened when you and Karen broke up." He sighed. "I mean, yeah, sometimes it sucks. There's this one guy at the bar who calls me a faggot and threatens to kick my ass every time he gets drunk, and probably he'll succeed one day. Half this damn country thinks we don't deserve all of our basic civil rights. And sometimes you have to be secretive about who you're fucking for your own safety. But I would guess, based on your general mood over the last few weeks, that you and Lowell have a good thing going. If he makes you happy, you can't just throw that away because you're scared."

Jase sat back on the couch. "Fine, so put the gay thing aside. I'm a package deal, remember? I can't just thrust him into instant fatherhood."

"Have you talked to him about this?"

"No."

"He likes Layla. Layla likes him. Right?"

"Yeah. Hell, she talks about him all the time these days."

Neal contemplated the coffee table. He looked up at Jase. "I'm not saying it will be easy. But give Lowell a chance. Maybe he doesn't want to be a father, but maybe he does. Maybe he cares enough about you that he's willing to try. Maybe this can all work out for you."

Jase dropped the bottle opener. He didn't know how to respond.

Neal frowned. "Look, you want to talk, I'm all ears."

"I don't want to talk anymore."

"Fair enough." Neal turned his attention back toward the TV. "Yanks scored two while you were out. That rookie you like hit a double and got two RBIs."

Jase tried to focus on the game, but mostly just saw colorful blurs moving on his television. He'd pissed Lowell off. He'd handled it badly. Then he remembered the expression on Lowell's face before he'd walked away and knew it was much worse than that. Lowell wasn't just angry; Jase had hurt him. And that was unforgivable.

But maybe it was for the best. Jase was falling for Lowell, so maybe it was better to end it now before he got any more emotionally invested. Lowell deserved more. He deserved better than to be with someone who was so terrified and fucked-up. Never mind that the mere thought of Lowell with any other man tore at Jase's heart.

He considered what Neal had said, but there was just no way. He felt completely overwhelmed. He wasn't ready. He couldn't do this. He wanted everything to go back the way it was before Lowell had moved into the house next door, before his whole life had gotten turned upside down. Maybe he hadn't been happy, but life had been so much simpler and easier.

He was thinking about Lowell when he felt the couch shake. Neal was cheering. "Holy shit, did you see that?"

Jase blinked several times. "What? Sorry, I spaced out."

Neal rolled his eyes. "Smoothest double play I've ever seen." Neal nudged Jase with his elbow. "You are so not okay."

"No. I don't think I am."

* * *

Lowell walked into Schuster's later that night and wondered if the venue choice was a mistake. He felt Neal watching him as he came into the bar. Then he berated himself for being so angsty about the situation. Sure, he and

Jase had come here together a number of times, but it was also one of the only decent bars in Greenbriar.

He sat right in front of where Neal stood. "How are you?" Neal asked.

"I've been better."

Joanie bustled in and sat next to Lowell. "I got here as soon as I could. You sounded awful on the phone. Are you all right? What happened?"

Neal plunked a snifter of some kind of alcohol in front of Lowell, but Lowell waved it off. "I'm not sure exactly. I think I got dumped?"

"Dumped? I didn't even know you were seeing anybody. You were seeing somebody? In Greenbriar?" At Lowell's nod, Joanie said quietly, "How many gay men can there really be in this town? The only ones I know of are you and Neal." She paused, and then she chuckled. "Unless you've been sleeping with a certain red-brief-wearing neighbor."

Lowell just looked at her. She smiled. Then she got it.

"No! Oh you are kidding me. Please tell me you're kidding."

Lowell cradled his face in his hands on the bar.

He heard Neal speak close to his ear. "For what it's worth, I don't think you're really dumped."

Lowell lifted his head far enough to look at Neal. "You know?

"Jase told me this afternoon, yeah. Under duress, for what it's worth."

Joanie put a hand on Lowell's back and rubbed a few times, which was a little bit comforting. "What happened?"

Lowell shrugged. "We hooked up for the first time in July. Things were, I thought, going really, really well, if a little intense."

"So he's bi? Gay? How did you know he's into guys? *Did* you know?"

Lowell shook his head. "I was pretty well convinced that he was straight, until this one night when we went out for pizza, and he started talking about his divorce, and it became obvious why his marriage fell apart. That night was the first time we...you know."

"And you fought this afternoon," Neal said.

Lowell put his head back in his arms. "He doesn't want to come out, basically. He says we can't ever be a real couple, that whatever was going on between us was just sex. Which is total bullshit, by the way. It's a lot more than that, and he knows it, but he's putting me off for what reason? So a couple of assholes in Greenbriar don't judge him?"

"There's a little more to it than that," Neal said.

Joanie shook her head. "I still can hardly believe this. Jase. Jason Midland. Star of the Greenbriar High School baseball team, king of the jocks. Once married to a woman, now devoted father. That Jason Midland."

Lowell was weary. "Please don't—"

"I won't tell anyone." She looked at Neal. "You knew?"

"Yeah, I knew. Although we never talked about it until this afternoon." He looked at the drink he'd poured for Lowell, then picked it up and took a sip. "Even if I hadn't been able to intuit it on my own, right around the time his divorce was final, we started going out a lot. Usually, we'd take the train down to the city. Sometimes Russ would come too, but more than half the time, it was just me and Jase. We'd go to these bars or these clubs that catered to a wide audience, or sometimes we'd even go to gay bars with Jase making the argument that he could pick up some guy's fag hag. The first few times, he'd say something like, 'I see a girl over there I'd like to get to know,' and then we'd split up and find each other later. Sometimes we'd split up for the night, take the train home separately. I'm sure you know what it's like, Lowell."

"I guess." He looked at Neal. "I think I've kind of outgrown the back rooms. The main advantage of being out is that you don't have to sneak around so much, you know?"

"I know. Why do you think I stopped bothering?" Neal sighed. "So Jase would vanish, and I'd mack on some guy. It seemed like a good arrangement. I had kind of suspected about Jase but thought he was still misguidedly going after women until one night when I saw him leave a club with a guy." Neal downed the rest of the drink. "I caught him a few other times too. He must have known I saw him. But we never spoke about it."

Lowell frowned. He wasn't surprised, but the situation made him feel deeply sad. "I guess that answers the question of who he's been with since Karen."

Neal refilled the glass. "He's punishing himself, is what he's doing. I suppose eighteen years of Father Anthony's sermons will warp your perceptions of what's decent and acceptable."

Lowell nodded. He'd gone to church with his mother often enough as a kid, mostly because if he was at church, he wasn't alone in the house with his father. He'd always kind of regarded religion as so much baloney, even if his mother seemed to believe it. Still, he could imagine that a susceptible kid—perhaps one who didn't have a father who was only too eager to beat any belief that there was a benevolent God right out of him—would internalize being told every Sunday that anyone who was not chaste and heterosexual was going to hell.

Neal went on, "I will grant you, he never should have married Karen to begin with. He knew going into the marriage. He spent most of the night before his wedding vomiting in my bathroom. I'm pretty sure he knew he was gay when he got married and did it anyway because he thought marriage would cure him, or at least that he could hide who he really was, I guess. He learned otherwise in time, and he's still punishing himself for misleading Karen. He thinks he deserves to be this unhappy."

Lowell shook his head. "He's depressed too. Just really unhappy with his job, with the house, with everything except Layla, and I want to help him, but I can't."

"I'm so sick of this," said Neal. "The situation is ridiculous. You know what the worst part is? You *were* helping him. He's been in this funk for years, before the divorce even. And I know that Jase really likes you. You can see it on his face whenever you're together. I haven't seen him smile like that in a long time. He smiles like he did when we were kids, when he was playing baseball." He looked like he was going to say more, but was interrupted by the door opening.

Russ came in and took the empty stool next to Lowell. "Hey guys. How's it going?"

Lowell managed to catch Neal's gaze and tilted his head toward Russ to ask if Russ knew about the situation. Neal shook his head almost imperceptibly.

"Hey, Russ," Neal said. He pulled a beer and placed it in front of Russ. Lowell thought it was an automatic gesture, one that came from habit and long friendship.

"Did I interrupt something?" Russ asked.

"Poor Lowell got his heart broken," Joanie said. "We were just comforting him."

"I'm sorry to hear that, man."

"Eh," said Lowell. The preceding conversation had only served to make him feel worse, but he didn't feel like he knew Russ well enough to have a little breakdown in front of him.

"How's Francesca?" Neal asked.

"She's okay," said Russ.

"Francesca Bianchi?" Joanie asked.

"Yeah, we've been kind of seeing each other for the last couple of weeks."

"Wow, really? I didn't think she was allowed to date anyone who wasn't Catholic."

"I could be Catholic," Russ said. "My parents are Catholic."

Neal laughed. "You, my friend, could never pull that off."

Joanie grinned. "Yeah, we sent this dweeby kid off to college, and *you* returned. They stop letting you be Catholic after so many premarital conquests."

Russ grunted. "It hasn't been going that well, anyway."

"Really?" said Neal.

Lowell looked at Neal, whose lips were pursed in anger. Lowell turned back at Russ, who was pouting a little.

Russ took a sip of his beer and said, "We can't all be studs all the time." He turned to Lowell. "It was a guy who broke your heart, right?"

"Yeah." Lowell wondered what Russ was getting at.

Russ nodded. "Men are assholes. I'm an asshole."

"I don't think we know each other well enough for me to pass judgment on you specifically, but I can't disagree with your general assertion there." He sighed. "It's fine. I'll be fine. It's not really over yet, right?"

"Sure, honey," Joanie said. She hugged him. "You care about him? I think you should fight for him."

"I agree," Neal said. "He's pushing you away because it's easier than facing what he's feeling. Don't let him do that."

Lowell nodded, starting to feel better for the first time all day. He could fight for Jase. He *would* fight, make Jase see all the things he could have, how happy they could be together.

"Who is this guy?" Russ asked.

"Nobody," everyone else said in unison.

Chapter Fourteen

Seven o'clock came and went without Karen dropping Layla off. Jase was worried. By eight, he was pacing around his house, feeling queasy, simultaneously trying to reassure himself that everything was fine and convince himself that they'd perished in a fire when Karen's car had gone off the road.

He called Karen's cell phone first and got no answer. Then he tried her parents' house. Her father said that Karen and Layla had come for dinner and left around six forty-five. "*I thought she was headed for your house*," he'd said.

Jase thanked his former father-in-law and then flipped on the TV to see if there had been any natural disasters he hadn't heard about yet. He tried Karen's cell phone again four times, getting her cheery, "Hiya, this is Karen, leave me a message!" greeting each time, which annoyed him a little more whenever he heard it.

He was tempted to hop in his car and drive around looking, but he didn't want to miss Karen and Layla if they were just late. He paced around his living room some more before calling the only other person he could think of to call.

Lowell answered after the second ring. "Hello?" *Thank goodness.*

On one breath, Jase said, "I know we argued this afternoon but Layla's not home yet and Karen's not answering her phone and I don't know if they're missing or if they went somewhere or what and I'm kind of freaking out—"

"Shh, stop, take a deep breath. Do you need my help?"

"Yes." He leaned his forehead against a wall. God, did he need Lowell. More than he'd ever be willing to admit aloud. "Please. Can you come here? I'm at home."

"I'm at Schuster's, but I can be there in fifteen minutes."

"Yeah. Um, can you keep an eye out too? Karen drives a silver Corolla."

"Yes, of course. I'll look. Sit tight, I'll be there soon."

"Okay. Thanks, Lowell."

"It's no problem."

It occurred to Jase after he hung up the phone that if Lowell was at Schuster's, he might have been drinking, which only kicked up his anxiety another notch, worried now that he'd cause a drunk-driving accident, and now Lowell was going to die in a fiery crash, and it was all Jase's fault.

But Lowell arrived at Jase's door in one piece fifteen minutes later as promised, looking sober. "Anything?" he asked.

"No, nothing. I tried her cell again, but she's not answering it."

Lowell kicked the door closed behind him, then stepped forward and took Jase into his arms. Jase leaned into him and realized that this was something significant, finding comfort in Lowell this way. Just having Lowell there eased his stress a little.

Jase put a little distance between them, though he didn't pull away entirely. He was conscious of the tension still between them. He shouldn't have expected to find anything like relief in Lowell's arms, not after the conversation they'd had that afternoon. The urgency of Layla being missing made it easy enough for him to put his focus back on the larger problem at hand. He'd have to find a way to deal with Lowell later. In the meantime, he was grateful for any help.

He related what Karen's parents had told him about her being on the way to his house at six forty-five. "It's almost nine. I'm going crazy here."

Lowell, for his part, seemed to be ignoring any problems between them as well. "We'll find them," he said. "Do you want me to drive around town some more, go look for them?"

"Would you?"

"Yeah. I'd hate for anything to have happened to Layla. Any special places I should look?"

"They might have gone to another movie. Or the mall in Danbury, maybe. I can't think of what else would be open at this time of night."

Lowell nodded. He seemed the picture of calm. He kissed Jase's forehead and eased out of his arms. Jase hadn't realized how hard he'd been holding on until Lowell gently lifted his hands away. "We'll find them," he said. Then he was out the door.

* * *

Lowell tried to be methodical, but it was hard to know where to even start when looking for a lost girl. He was pretty sure there was a rational explanation for Karen and Layla's disappearance, that maybe Karen had just decided to take Layla shopping, or they'd driven around or something. Hadn't Jase said Karen was flakey?

He drove to Danbury, keeping his eyes peeled for a silver Corolla. His mind also kept wandering to the fight he and Jase had had that afternoon, if it could even be called a fight. He thought about some of the things Neal had told him that evening, as well. The situation seemed impossible. Jase wasn't willing to be in a relationship with him because of shame or pride or self-loathing. Lowell knew deep down that he deserved better than to be Jase's secret piece on the side. But that didn't stop him from wanting Jase.

He hadn't arrived at any conclusion about Layla besides that he really liked the kid. Could he be a stepfather? He liked kids okay but had never really wanted any of his own. A relationship with Jase, if Jase ever got over his fear—which seemed like a big *if*—would mean that Lowell would have to take on some kind of parental responsibility, would have to take care of Layla. Could he do that? Did he want to?

He realized as he drove that he hadn't even given his decision to help find Layla a moment's thought. He'd just done it, almost by instinct. His worry for her and Jase had been foremost on his mind. It still made him nervous sometimes, what might be expected of him if Jase ever got over himself, and they had a real relationship. The fact that it might not work out that way made Lowell suddenly sad. He wouldn't just be losing Jase; he'd be losing Layla as well. Assuming they hadn't already lost her, he thought. He refocused his attention back on driving.

He supposed the fact that he was driving all over western Connecticut to find that same little girl answered his question.

"Dammit, Jase," he whispered to his empty car.

He hadn't seen any silver cars at all by the time he pulled into the parking lot. It was almost nine thirty, the time when the mall closed. He considered running inside and doing a lap through the building. He'd spent so much time here with Joanie when they were teenagers that he knew he could probably still navigate the thing. But part of him just knew Karen and Layla were not here. To be absolutely sure, he drove around the parking lot, he drove a lap around every level of the parking garage, and he drove to the strip mall next to the mall. No silver Corolla. He pulled over and called Jase.

"Anything?" Lowell asked.

"No, still can't get her on the phone. You haven't seen her yet?"

"Nope. I'm in Danbury. I've been driving around the parking lots around the mall for ten minutes. The mall just closed. Hardly anybody's here. I haven't seen her car. Any chance she's in a different car? What do her parents have?"

"Her father drives a big Caddy. It's black, I think, or really dark blue. Karen always complains about it, though, says she wouldn't be caught dead in that car. Her mom doesn't own a car anymore, has terrible eyesight."

"Okay." Lowell sighed. "I don't think I saw a Caddy, but I'll look for that too, just in case. There's no sign of them here. I'm gonna try Brookfield, go by all those strip malls, maybe go up as far as the Y. Then I'll turn around and do a loop through Greenbriar and I'll come back to your house."

"Sure," Jase said, sounding distracted.

"How are you doing?"

Jase made a strangled sound in his throat. "Where's my little girl? Why can't I find her?"

"I don't know. Just…try to hang on until I get back. I'm looking. I will do whatever I can. Okay?"

"Yeah. I'm gonna get off the phone in case they call."

Lowell put the car back in gear and drove to Brookfield.

* * *

When Lowell got back, an hour and a half after he'd left, Jase couldn't do anything more than sit on the couch, feeling anchored there. As if he knew that, Lowell walked right into the house without ringing the bell. He sat next to Jase.

"The good news is that a silver Corolla is not as common a car as you'd think," Lowell said.

"Should I call the police?"

"I don't know."

Jase was just barely keeping it together, overwhelmed with worry and now anger, the thought seeping into his consciousness that Karen had done something, taken Layla somewhere, put her in a dangerous situation. "I called Karen's parents again. She hasn't come home. Her dad went out to go look too. They live over in Bethel."

"That's another set of eyes at least."

Jase nodded. He buried his face in his hands. He felt a hand on his back, rubbing gently. He let himself get pulled into Lowell's arms and found a little bit of comfort there.

His cell phone rang.

Jase pushed Lowell away in an effort to get to it quickly. The caller ID said it was Karen. He flipped open the phone. "Where the hell are you?"

"Layla is with me, and she's safe," Karen said, "which is more than I'd be able to say for her if I'd dropped her back off at your house."

"What are you talking about? Where are you? You should have been back here hours ago."

"How could you, Jason?

"How could I what? Are you on your way here?"

"We agreed that you would not have any of your…indiscretions, and you certainly wouldn't expose Layla to any of it."

"What are you talking about? Expose Layla to what?"

"Layla saw you kissing that man!"

"What?" Jase couldn't think of when Layla would have seen them. "What does this have to do with anything? Bring Layla back!"

"She told me she saw you and Lowell kiss. She was very upset about it."

"I doubt she was upset. She didn't say anything to me." He wanted to start making demands, but he worried that if he pushed Karen too hard, she'd never bring Layla back.

There was a pause before Karen said, "So you did kiss him."

It seemed futile to deny it. "Yes, I did."

"Jason."

"You told me you didn't want me to expose Layla to any of the men I went out with. I haven't. Lowell is my neighbor, and he was my friend before there was any kissing." Lowell turned to look at him when he heard his name. His eyes were wide.

"Are you involved with him?"

"I kept it away from Layla, just like you asked."

"Not if she saw you kissing."

"I can't imagine when she saw it. When did she see us kiss?"

"She didn't say exactly. Just 'the other night.'"

Jase thought about it and reasoned it had to be the night when Lowell had dropped off his jacket, when they'd kissed in the living room while Jase thought Layla was getting ready for bed. "I didn't realize… It won't happen again."

Lowell frowned and shook his head.

Frustrated, Jase said, "I don't see the point of this. It's late, well past Layla's bedtime. Bring her home!"

"I won't. I will not let her into that house with you. You're a pervert, and you broke your promise. I've had enough of letting you control how we raise our daughter. I'm just as good a parent as you are, and just because I don't have everything figured out doesn't mean only you should get custody. I don't think you should have custody at all."

Jase suddenly felt very tired. There was some relief in hearing that Layla was all right, that they hadn't in fact perished in a horrific car crash. He was also tired of having this fight with Karen.

"There were papers, Karen," Jase said, knowing how weary the words sounded. He took a deep breath to muster every bit of calm he could. "We agreed. Layla would live with me. You signed away custody because we agreed it was the right thing. And I've complied with every part of our agreement. She sees your parents once a month. You can visit with her as often as you want. And it's always you who reneges. You're the one who schedules visits but doesn't show up for them. You're the one who makes promises she doesn't keep. I know you love her, but you can't do this. I didn't do anything wrong here."

"I got fucked in the divorce, Jason. Isn't that ironic? You refused to fuck me in bed, so you fucked me with lawyers. You at least had a place to go. I had nothing. Nowhere to go, no job. I stopped working to raise Layla, remember?"

"That was your choice."

"That you encouraged. And now nothing is good. Nothing is going well. I can't get work, I live with my fucking parents part of the time, and I can't even see my own daughter most of the time. How is that fair? And for what? We were supposed to be together forever, Jason. That's what marriage means. Instead, you forced me out. Because you think you're..." She drew a sharp breath.

"Gay. I'm gay. I wish that things were different, but they aren't. Believe me, I wish things were different. But I'm learning to accept that this is who I am. I wish that you would too."

"I don't know if I can. And I won't make Layla accept it, either. It's too bad it had to come to this, but if you're going to carry on like you have been, then I can't bring her back to your house."

He wiped sweat from his brow. "Where are you?"

"Far from Greenbriar. Layla and I are taking a vacation."

"Karen, you can't do this. Turn the car around, come here. Bring Layla back home."

"No. I'm her parent now. See that, I'm doing you a favor! Now you can fuck all the men you want, you asshole."

Jase was stunned. He wondered if he should have seen this coming, but part of him couldn't believe that Karen would actually do something like this.

He took a deep breath. "Fine, okay. You win. Just…bring her back to me. I won't see Lowell anymore, I won't—"

"What was it you told me when I moved out? You can't change your nature. You can't help the fact that you never really found me attractive, that our whole marriage was a sham. Even if it's not this man, it'll be another man, and I can't let my daughter into an environment like that. Layla and I, we're going to move to a new state and start over."

"How? You don't have any money."

"I have some!"

"You just asked me to borrow money a few weeks ago!"

"Don't worry about it. Go back to fucking your *boyfriend.*"

"Karen…"

"Bye, Jason." She hung up.

Jase couldn't breathe. Then, suddenly, Lowell was kneeling on the floor in front of him. "What did she say?"

"Karen took her," Jase said. "She doesn't think I can be gay and be a good parent, so she took Layla." He looked at Lowell, saw the concern there, and felt pain in his chest. "What am I going to do?"

Lowell stood up and picked up the house phone. Jase heard him dial a few numbers, then realized he'd called 9-1-1. Jase pulled his knees up onto the couch and laid his head on the armrest. The hopelessness of the situation struck him all at once, and he wondered how to negotiate this, what he would have to do if he got Layla back. He'd give up Lowell. He'd give up sex. He'd move out of the house if he had to.

Anything to bring back his little girl.

Anything.

Chapter Fifteen

Lowell recognized a kindred spirit in Detective Sam Brown. He was plain-looking, with tousled, mousy-brown hair and an unremarkable face, but he looked strong and there was an undeniable intelligence in his tired eyes. He showed up at Jase's door wearing a T-shirt and jeans. His badge hung from a chain around his neck. Given that it was close to midnight by the time he arrived, Lowell guessed someone had chased him out of bed. Something about his stance pinged Lowell's gaydar too, but he decided that was neither here nor there.

"You're not Jason Midland," he said when Lowell answered the door.

"No, Lowell Fisher. I live next door. Jase is in the living room."

The detective nodded. "Sam Brown. I graduated two years ahead of you," he said. "From Greenbriar High, I mean."

"Oh." Lowell wished he remembered. Greenbriar had not been that big of a school, only about 800 students in all, but Sam Brown had one of those faces that would have gotten lost in any crowd. Lowell flipped through his mental yearbook and came up empty. Still, he said, "Shame we have to meet again under these circumstances."

"Surprised it took this long. I arrested your father a couple of times."

Lowell sighed. "Yeah. I imagine he kept you guys pretty busy."

"I was sorry to hear he died, for what it's worth."

Lowell shrugged. "Not why we're here."

The detective followed Lowell into the living room. Jase hadn't gotten off the couch since Lowell had gotten back from his drive around town. He seemed to be in a state of shock, unable to speak much. He'd tried to call Karen back a couple of times, still only getting her voicemail, and after the last time, he'd thrown his cell phone across the room with such force that it hit the wall, cracking the screen. When Jase looked at the broken screen, he was inconsolable.

"Jase," Lowell said. "This is Detective Brown."

Jase looked up.

"Call me Sam."

Jase uncurled enough to offer a hand.

"So what happened?" Sam asked.

Jase and Lowell tag-teamed to explain what was going on, leaving out the fact that they'd been having an affair. Kindred spirit or not, Lowell wasn't ready to volunteer that information, especially considering the argument with Jase that afternoon. That argument seemed like it had happened three days ago.

Sam made some notes on a pad of paper. "Any idea why your ex-wife would kidnap your daughter?"

Jase shook his head. "I think she thinks she can be a better parent? I don't know." In the barest of terms, Jase explained their custody agreement, how Karen had essentially signed over her rights when the divorce was final because Jase was more stable. "Nothing in her life has really changed at all, but she just got this idea in her head that I'm a bad parent now."

"Why does she think that?"

Jase did a decent job of looking bewildered by this turn of events.

Sam looked to Lowell for an explanation. It seemed unfair to leave Sam in the dark, but their affair didn't seem relevant to the actual fact of Karen having run off.

"Well," Sam said, running a hand through his disheveled hair, "it's not the first time I've seen a case like this. We handled a similar situation last year. Mom had won full custody in the divorce, Dad picked up their kid from school one day, then took off. Teacher didn't know they'd divorced, didn't know it wasn't okay for Dad to pick up the kid."

"Did you get the kid back?" Jase asked.

"Yeah. Dad used his credit card to pay for some fast food at a rest stop in New Jersey. He wasn't hard to track down after that."

That seemed to ease Jase's worry a little.

They talked for a while longer, Sam writing down all of Karen's specifics. They worked together to make a list of places Karen might have gone—Jase thought she might have gone north, because she had family in Massachusetts and Vermont and a lot of friends in the Boston area. The idea was floated that she might even drive to Canada, which would make getting her back a lot more difficult. Sam said he'd start work on the case right away. When he left, he promised to call as soon as he made any progress.

Lowell sat next to Jase again after Sam left. "Do you want me to get something for you? Glass of water? I could make coffee."

"You should probably leave," Jase said.

"It's fine, I'll stay as long as you need me."

Jase frowned. "I think what I need is for you to leave."

"Jase…"

"Let me explain," he said, with surprising calm. "When we divorced, I promised Karen I'd keep my private life away from Layla. I agreed, essentially, that I wouldn't have a relationship with a man, or if I did, that I wouldn't bring him home. I didn't think this would be a big problem. I never brought anyone home and never wanted to."

"Until now."

Jase squirmed in his seat. "I never expected… Well, I never thought I'd ever even have the chance to be with someone like you. And Karen, well. I know this isn't about you specifically or even about me being gay. She's still angry and hurt, and she's in the right because I lied to her. I lied to myself." He rubbed his forehead. "So tonight she called me a pervert and took our daughter away. Layla is the most important thing in my life. She has been since the day I found out she was on the way, and she always will be. Nothing changes that. I know in my gut that she is better off living with me than she is with Karen, that this house, this town, is what is best for her. And I want her with me, I don't want to miss any moment of her life unless I have to, and it kills me a little every time she goes off with Karen."

"I know," Lowell said. He did know that. It became abundantly clear all at once that he hadn't really thought through what getting involved with a man with a child would entail. He'd never expected to lose to the kid, but that's exactly what was happening. And that was fair. It was hard to blame Jase. Layla was his daughter and should come first. Lowell was…well, nothing specific to Jase. Certainly not his boyfriend. He was the neighbor. The sometimes friend. The fuck buddy.

Lowell knew what they had went deeper than that, knew he meant more to Jase than Jase would ever let on. He knew also that he couldn't compete with Layla, nor should he. If Jase had to make a choice, the choice was obvious.

"I'm sorry," Jase whispered.

Lowell moved toward the door. "I know you won't, but try to get some sleep. I'll be around tomorrow if you need anything. Okay? Call anytime."

"Yeah," Jase said.

Lowell knew he wouldn't call or stop by. He nodded, feeling the finality in this. He leaned over and kissed Jase. It was a good-bye kiss, meant to be comforting, but Jase's fingers curled into his shirt, held on. Lowell had to get out of the house before he got his heart completely destroyed. He backed away and left.

* * *

Jase spent the entire night awake, staring at the cordless extension of the house phone, which he had propped up on the nightstand. No one called.

When he deemed it late enough in the morning for it to be appropriate, he called his former in-laws to see if they'd heard anything.

Karen's parents had never especially liked him. He figured they knew from the beginning what he wouldn't have been able to admit to himself. The divorce hadn't exactly endeared him to them, either. They hadn't been outright hostile to him, knowing well enough that pissing him off would limit how often they saw their granddaughter, but they were often cold to him, and this phone call was no exception.

"Karen did call us last night," her father, Richard, said. "She explained what happened. Frankly, I'm not feeling that inclined to help you. If I had known you were exposing *my* granddaughter…"

"I have legal custody," Jase said weakly. "The police are investigating. They will track Karen down soon enough."

"Your house is not a good place for Layla to be."

Jase wanted to make the gay-not-a-pedophile argument, but didn't have the energy for it. "She belongs here," he said instead. "I've never done anything to put Layla in any kind of danger. If Karen brings Layla back, I swear, I won't ever…" He didn't want to finish the thought.

"Good-bye, Jase." Richard hung up.

A little while later, he got a call from Sam Brown. "Nothing on any of Karen's cards," he said, "but there was a motel room charged to her father's card. Seeing as how I spoke with him on his home phone last night, I'm guessing he wasn't the one renting a room."

"Where was the hotel room?"

"Over near Poughkeepsie. I called a guy I know on the PD there, but by the time they got to the motel, your ex-wife had already cleared out."

"Shit."

"You told me yourself that her finances are not good. If she keeps using this credit card, we'll be able to track her and catch up with her soon."

"Okay."

"We'll get your daughter back, Mr. Midland."

Jase liked the conviction in Sam's voice. "Thank you."

"I know you're worried. I'll be in touch."

Neal came by late morning with coffee and doughnuts. He tried to distract Jase with talk of baseball, but Jase's heart wasn't in it. Mostly, they sat on the couch with the TV on in the background without saying much, though Jase appreciated that Neal was trying. He didn't especially want to be alone, either. Neal had to leave midafternoon to go tend to Schuster's. By then, Jase hadn't heard much from the police and was half out of his mind. He was pacing around his living room again when the doorbell rang again.

"Any news?" Lowell asked.

Jase couldn't face Lowell now, didn't know how to handle him, but let him in anyway. "Nothing," he said. "She seems to be moving west, but the police haven't caught up with her yet."

To his credit, Lowell knit his eyebrows together, and he reached over and laid a comforting hand on Jase's arm. Jase took a step back, out of Lowell's grasp. He knew that he could easily fall into those arms, and it was almost physically impossible to keep the distance between them, but he had to maintain some space, or he'd never be able to let Lowell go. Lowell lowered his hand but pursed his lips.

"You should leave," Jase said.

"I understand that, but I can help. You shouldn't have to sit here and fret by yourself. I just figure, if you need someone to sit with you while you wait, to hold your hand, I'm your man."

"I'll call Neal or someone."

Lowell's face twisted in pain. "I'm not trying to get into your pants, Jase. I'm trying to be your *friend*."

"Don't you think we went way past that a while ago?"

Lowell's eyebrows shot up. "Oh *now* you're willing to acknowledge there's more to our relationship."

Jase took a step back. "Well, if it hadn't been for our relationship, none of this would have happened."

"What are you talking about?"

Jase threw his hands in the air. "I was never looking for a boyfriend! I just wanted to get laid! I was attracted to you, and I went for it, and then everything became this big ratfuck."

Lowell pinched the bridge of his nose. When he looked up, there were dark circles under his eyes. Jase wondered if he had also spent a sleepless night, if he'd been up fretting over Layla or Jase himself, but that was too much to contemplate just then.

Lowell said, "You're scared."

"Shit, yeah, I'm scared!" Jase found his control breaking. "This is all because of you! Everything was fine before you moved back to Greenbriar. Karen and I could have gone on forever the way we were, and then Layla would still be here. She'd be safe. "

"So, what? You would have just gone to the city, hooked up with some random dude to get your needs met, then come back to Connecticut to play doting dad? That's a pretty fucked-up way to live."

"But it was working, wasn't it? Everything was fine. Then I got involved with you, and now my daughter is God knows where."

Lowell shook his head. "This was Karen's doing. It had nothing to do with me or us. She's the one who acted. She's the one who took Layla."

"She wouldn't have done it if it hadn't been for you. You and I should never have gotten involved."

Lowell stared at the floor for a long moment before he turned and walked to the door. He turned back before he left and said, "You know, after we fought yesterday, I had decided that I would fight for you. I know you think you can't have everything that will make you happy, but I was determined to show you that you could. We could be great together. I know you know that. I saw it on your face, in your eyes, when we were together. Hell, you said it yourself, that being with me made you happy. But if you're so goddamned determined to throw it all away, then I don't see the point in fighting for you."

"Fuck you, Lowell. This is about Layla, not you. How can you be so selfish?"

"It doesn't have to be a contest. You shouldn't have to choose between her and me. Until five minutes ago, you could have had us both, but I'm done arguing. I don't have it in me. I'm sorry it had to be this way. Good-bye." He put his hand on the doorknob.

"Good-bye," Jase said. He felt like he'd been hit in the head with a baseball bat. This was what he wanted, wasn't it? For his life to go back to the way it had been before Lowell had come back into it. Then why did it feel so much like he'd just hit rock bottom?

Lowell turned back and looked at Jase. He sighed. "Would you...?"

Jase felt the fight drain out of him. "What?"

"When Layla comes back, could you just give me a call, let me know she's all right? I promise I'll leave you alone after that."

Jase didn't know why Lowell would want that, but he said, "Yeah, okay."

Lowell nodded. He seemed reluctant to leave. A storm of emotion raged in Jase. He was so angry: at Karen, at Lowell, at the situation, at everything. But part of him wasn't quite ready to let Lowell go yet, either. Intellectually, he knew that Lowell meant well, but Jase knew also that none of this would have happened if not for Lowell's return and Jase's weakness where Lowell was concerned. He was being pulled in two directions. He couldn't stand the sight of Lowell. But he needed Lowell. That need propelled him forward, and he put his hand over Lowell's where it rested on the doorknob.

"I should leave," Lowell said. "I need to leave."

"I can't do this."

"Have me, or let me leave?"

"Either." Jase closed the distance between them and kissed him. Lowell didn't move except to lean into the kiss. Jase started to back away, intending to let Lowell leave, but he couldn't bring himself to let go entirely. "I can't."

"You want me to stay."

Jase looked down, unable to speak. What he wanted didn't matter anymore. What he wanted wasn't possible.

"You can't go back, you know," Lowell said quietly. "Pushing me out the door, that won't fix your life."

"I know. Keeping you here doesn't fix it either."

"Jase—"

They kissed again—Jase couldn't be sure who kissed whom, as their lips just seemed to find their way to each other—and this time, Jase pulled Lowell's hand off the doorknob and placed it on his waist. Lowell mumbled a protest but didn't pull away.

Jase just wanted one more time with Lowell. He wanted one last memory, something he could think about instead of their last fight. And he wanted Lowell to help him forget, to distract him until there was news of Karen and Layla, because sitting around waiting for it was driving him mad.

They kept kissing, and Jase pulled Lowell toward the couch. "This is not a good idea," Lowell said. He kissed Jase again.

"I know." Jase grabbed the hem of Lowell's T-shirt and pulled it off over his head. Having sex with Lowell while Layla was missing, while he was angry at Lowell, while Lowell was hurt and angry too, was a phenomenally stupid idea. But that didn't stop Jase from pursuing it.

They kissed as Jase sat on the couch and pulled Lowell down with him. Jase kept his eyes shut, not willing to look at Lowell, just wanting to feel, to pretend. He felt Lowell's hands, the wide palms and long fingers—unmistakably a man's hands—moving under his shirt, over his skin, sliding up his torso. His shirt was pulled off, but he didn't open his eyes.

He writhed and arched as Lowell started nibbling down his neck, over his chest, and then teeth clamped down on a nipple. Jase nearly leaped off the couch. Lowell's fingers dug into his flesh, hard enough to leave bruises, and it hurt, but it was real. As Lowell's mouth moved over his skin, he felt like he was being devoured.

The words, "Kiss me," slipped out of Jase's mouth before it was even a conscious desire in his mind. Lowell complied, and the devouring continued. Lowell's teeth scraped against Jase's lips and tongue. Jase wanted to be close to Lowell and pushed inside, his tongue sliding against the top of Lowell's mouth. Lowell groaned and rocked his hips. Jase wanted Lowell so badly, so acutely, wanted more than anything for Lowell to make love to him or else turn him over and fuck him over the side of the couch—Jase couldn't decide which would be better.

Maybe he wouldn't have to decide, he thought. Maybe he could just have Lowell, keep him here, in this moment. He thought of all the times they'd had sex and then lingered in Lowell's bed afterward, how safe it felt there, like the outside world couldn't get to him. He thought maybe he could find safety like that here, in his own living room, in Lowell's arms. He undid Lowell's jeans and slid his hands inside, felt the warmth of skin before he felt Lowell's heavy erection against his palms. He wanted it inside him; he wanted to be wrapped up in Lowell. He needed Lowell, he wanted Lowell, and he knew, in that moment, that he loved Lowell.

Jase wrapped his hands around Lowell's cock, and Lowell cried out. He pushed Lowell's pants down his hips, exposing the smooth skin of his ass. Lowell kissed him and undid his pants, and it was like relief when their erections finally rubbed against each other. Jase gasped, the heat between them like a fire that consumed everything in its wake. His skin felt like it was burning.

"Just like this," Lowell murmured, thrusting against him.

Every movement was electric. Jase couldn't get over how goddamned *good* this felt, to be in Lowell's arms, to even just rub against him, his body, his skin. Jase bucked and arched as heat and tremors poured through him, as Lowell's movements pushed him closer to the cliff. He clawed at Lowell, shoving his hands under Lowell's shirt, pulling it off, to get his fingers on his skin, digging his nails into Lowell's back.

Lowell gasped, then muttered, "Shit." Jase felt Lowell's cock pulse against his own, then Lowell's cum splashed hot against his stomach. Lowell's orgasm triggered his own, and he shouted Lowell's name. He thrust his hips against Lowell's, and the orgasm ripped through him. He exploded against Lowell, clutching at his skin.

When everything subsided, he slumped against the couch as Lowell collapsed on top of him, and all of the energy seemed to drain from his body.

The phone rang.

Lowell jumped away, recoiling as if in horror, and then he was off the couch. He hurriedly buttoned up his jeans, then picked up his shirt. Jase swallowed and grabbed the phone.

"Hello?"

"It's Sam. Karen used her father's credit card in Rhinebeck, at a gas station. We think she's traveling up Route Nine, possibly toward Albany. Does she know anyone in the area?"

Jase's head still swam with Lowell. He could feel and smell Lowell on his skin. Hell, the man himself was standing in the middle of the living room, staring at him with an expression of shock and maybe disgust on his face. Jase had to fight to get his thinking back on Karen. "We went to college with a guy who I think lives in Troy now."

"What's his name?"

Jase rattled off the names of everyone he knew who lived upstate. He watched Lowell put his shirt on. Lowell gestured toward the door and whispered, "I'm leaving."

Jase shook his head. He mouthed, "Wait," then focused back on Sam. "What can I do?"

"I hate to say this, but for now all you can do is wait. The New York State Thruway Police are on this too. Everyone's looking. We'll find them."

"Can't you issue an AMBER Alert or something?"

"I want to, but it's pending approval by authorities in both Connecticut and New York. One of the criteria is that the child has to be considered in danger of serious injury or death. Even you don't think that's the case here, do you? Your ex-wife is trying to prove something, or she wants custody of your daughter, but she doesn't intend to do her any harm."

Jase felt queasy. He hadn't actually considered it a possibility that Karen might harm Layla. But now that the idea had entered his head, he couldn't erase it. Still, deep down, he didn't think that was the objective here. Karen thought she was saving Layla. "No, you're right. I don't think Karen intends to hurt Layla. Not intentionally, anyway. But she doesn't really have any money, and if they're just running... I mean, it's not really safe, right?"

"Yes, I agree. Okay. I'm doing everything I can. I just wanted to give you an update. I'll call again if I learn anything new."

"Yes. Thank you, Sam. I appreciate it."

"Just doing my job."

When Sam was off the phone, Jase put the receiver down and looked at Lowell, who had gone back to standing next to the door and looking pensive.

"Now I'm really going to leave," he said. "You have to focus on finding Layla."

He was right, of course. Jase felt suddenly horrified. What did having sex with Lowell accomplish when Layla was missing? He looked at the floor.

"I hope you find her. I really hope she's okay, and she makes it home to you. I can't do this, though. I can't pretend that things are right with us. Us having sex now, it doesn't change anything. Does it?"

"No." Because it didn't. He looked up. "You're right, it doesn't solve our problems."

Lowell was visibly upset, his eyebrows raised, his eyes looking tired. "I can't stand here and have you look at me the way that way, the way you have been since yesterday. Like I'm the reason Layla's not here."

"But if you hadn't…" And then Jase was angry again. The fact that none of this would have happened without Lowell was inescapable. And Jase clearly had not learned his lesson, if he was willing to do what they had just done on the couch. The new stain on Lowell's shirt didn't escape his notice, either, and he felt completely disgusted, though whether it was with Lowell or himself, he wasn't sure. More at me, he thought, because I can't stay away. "If we hadn't just…"

Lowell held up his hand. "I know. I don't want to fight about this more. If you can't see…" He looked up, a plea in his eyes.

"I need…" He wasn't sure what he needed. He needed Layla. A part of him needed Lowell too. But more than anything, he needed his life back to normal. "I need things to be back the way they were before I met you."

He regretted the words almost as soon as they were out of his mouth, because the hurt on Lowell's face was so clear, Jase felt it like a punch in the gut. Then Lowell recovered, making his face neutral. He nodded. "That's what I thought." He frowned and finally succeeded in turning the doorknob and opening the door.

Then he was gone.

198   Kate McMurray

Chapter Sixteen

As he drove his mother to her doctor's appointment the next day, Lowell thought he was a selfish asshole. He felt awful for trying to get a decision out of Jase, for trying to make Jase see this situation for what it was when he was so thoroughly distracted by what was happening with Layla. Even so, he'd seen the futility in fighting for their relationship now. It was maybe over for good if Jase was so hell-bent on blaming Lowell for what happened to Layla. He tried to tell himself that it wasn't worth fighting for a relationship that Jase had decided had no future.

He'd called Joanie after he'd left Jase's house, but when she had volunteered to come over, he put her off, deciding he'd prefer to wallow alone. Besides, life went on. He had other things to attend to, including taking his mother to the doctor.

The appointment seemed to go well, but Lowell thought that this was true primarily because his mother was clearheaded. She told the doctor about losing her keys, about being occasionally forgetful. The doctor drew blood and ran some other tests. As they were leaving, Lowell pulled the doctor aside. "Tell me straight. Is it Alzheimer's?"

"It's too soon for me to tell. We'll know better after she sees the neural specialist. But, between us? Yeah, I think it might be."

"Shit." It was almost too overwhelming to deal with. Losing Layla, losing Jase, and now he was probably losing his mother. It took a lot to maintain his composure with the doctor, but the man seemed to understand. He patted Lowell's arm.

"There are some medications that will help her stay alert, that will help with the memory loss. And it may be that you're right, and she's just still struggling with your father's death, and this will get better in a few months. But I think you have to prepare yourself for the possibility that this is something serious, which means you'll have to think about at-home care, or moving her out of her house."

"Yeah," Lowell said.

The doctor escorted Lowell to the waiting room. "We'll talk again after you see the specialist, all right? It could be this is nothing, just memory loss from aging. It happens to the best of us." The doctor smiled.

Lowell's mother nodded. Lowell took her outside and helped her into his car. "You want to go back to my house and have some tea?" Lowell asked. He found that he quite preferred having her come to his house. There were fewer ghosts there. Not to mention that he wanted to keep an eye on his neighbor's house, in the event Layla was returned.

"Yes, that would be nice."

She looked troubled. Lowell reached over and touched her hand. "Mom, it's going to be okay. We'll figure this out. I'm here to take care of you. Try not to worry."

She shot him a weak smile. "Thank you." They drove most of the way back in silence. When they were close to Lowell's house, she said, "Maybe it's a blessing. Maybe it's better not to remember."

Lowell opted not to comment. When they got to the house, he brought her inside. She still looked upset, but she took a deep breath and smiled at him. "Did you remember to buy honey this time?"

"Yes, Mom. And if you're feeling really daring, I bought this peach tea that I think is pretty good. You want to give that a try?"

"Why not?"

He put the pot on to boil. He glanced out his east-facing window, which gave him an unobstructed view of Jase's backyard. No little girl running there, like there should have been.

He thought about Jase offering to help him with his mother. It was a nice offer. Lowell had thought it sweet at the time, but Lowell couldn't accept help. All those years of relying on himself, of keeping that secret, of not letting anyone help him, it almost felt like habit. It was hard to let Jase help him, contacts or not. And maybe that was something else worth considering, if he'd ever be able to rely on someone else, if he could really make a family with Jase, if he could really trust him with his problems.

Of course, now was not the time to worry about that, since Layla was missing. More to the point, it was becoming increasingly likely that Lowell wouldn't even have the opportunity to make that family with Jase. Funny how now that the option was taken away, he wanted it more than anything.

"You look worried about something," his mother said, "and I don't think it's just me."

Lowell went to the cabinets and pulled out a couple of mugs. "It's Layla. You know, Jason Midland's daughter? His ex-wife took off with her last night. He hasn't been able to find them yet."

"God, that's awful. Has he called the police?"

"Yeah, they're tracking her north but haven't caught up with her yet."

"Why would she do that?"

Lowell wasn't sure how best to explain. "I don't..." Then he sighed. "Well, Jase and I were involved." He waited for his mother to react. Her eyebrows rose, but then she nodded. Lowell continued, "His ex-wife found out. She is a little homophobic. Or a lot homophobic, if she thought taking off with Layla was better than leaving her with Jase."

His mother shook her head. Lowell's orientation had not been a topic of conversation between him and his mother since he came back to Greenbriar. He guessed it would become one now. Then she surprised him. "She should have a gay son. Then she will learn."

"Mom." He handed her a mug and a tea bag, then placed a mug on the table for himself.

"I didn't know anything before you were born. And your father, well, you know how he was. He'd make fun of any man he thought was a sissy, and I used to laugh right along with him."

Lowell winced. He didn't want to hear this.

She reached over and touched his arm. "I listened when the priest said it was wrong, but then I watched you grow up. I kind of suspected... I mean, even before you told us. At first, I thought maybe you were just rebelling or trying to make your father angry, but I knew the truth, deep down. I thought about what I'd always been told, but then I thought that there was no way *my* son could be wrong. Not the innocent little boy I knew or even the troubled teenager. There was never anything wrong with you."

"But—"

"You're a good person, Lowell. You came back here to take care of me even though I know you didn't want to." She looked out the window. "I didn't know Jason was gay also, but I suppose that explains why he's not married anymore."

"Yeah." He frowned. His mother so rarely talked about anything personal, and her being candid made him a little uncomfortable. So he changed the subject. "Well, so, I guess I'm worried about Layla too. She's only six." The kettle wailed, so he picked it up and poured hot water into both mugs. Then he sat next to his mother.

He wasn't sure how much he should say. He supposed that his secret was out, and he wanted to kick himself for thinking that his mother might not even remember this conversation. He hoped she would remember, that she'd remember every conversation they'd had over tea.

If nothing else, he knew now that, without a doubt, he was in love with Jase, and there was not a damn thing he could do about it. He was pretty sure Jase felt the same way. And wasn't that a kick in the ass?

He realized that his mother was staring at him.

"You and Jason are not still together."

Lowell sighed. "No, not anymore."

"But you love him."

"Yes."

"And you love that little girl too, don't you?"

He hadn't thought about it before, but now that she mentioned it... "Yes, I do. But it doesn't matter because of this mess with his ex-wife, so it's over and I have to make my peace with that."

"That hardly seems fair," she said.

"Yeah, well. Life is not fair. You wound up with Dad."

"Lowell."

He shrugged.

"He loved you in his way," she said.

"What way is that? People do not express their love with their fists. He was ashamed of me."

"I hope you know I never was ashamed of you. And you've grown into a good man, despite the mistakes I made." She put an arm around his shoulders and squeezed before retreating again. "I wish I'd had the strength to leave your father. Jason had the strength to leave his wife, but it's not easy to keep moving forward. When this is resolved, when he has his daughter back, he'll get there."

"What if he doesn't?"

"Then you move on. You have opportunities that I never had. You are so smart and successful. You make enough money to live in this great house. You can get by on your own. You have a good heart. You will find someone who loves you. I want that for you so much."

"Thanks, Mom."

"I wish it had been different. I wish I could have taken you and run away from your father, but I just couldn't. I didn't have any money of my own, and he probably would have found me anyway. Instead I let him drive you away. That is my greatest regret. You are my son, Lowell, and I love you. I always have."

"I love you too," said Lowell.

* * *

The phone pulled Jase into wakefulness, and as he reached for his phone, he made the surprising realization that he'd fallen asleep. The display was cracked, but apparently the phone still worked.

"Hello?"

"Daddy?"

Jase stopped breathing. His chest seized up, and he gasped when he remembered that he had to inhale. "Oh Layla. I am so happy to hear your voice. Where is your mother?"

"She's asleep. I took her phone."

Jase picked up the house phone and dialed the number Sam Brown had given him.

"Layla, do you know where you are?"

"Brown," Sam said in the house extension.

"Sam," Jase whispered into the house phone. "Layla called my cell. I've got her on the line right now. Can you trace the call?"

"I'll see what I can do. Try to keep her on the line as long as possible."

Jase went back to the cell phone. Jase was grateful he'd taken the time to make Layla memorize his cell phone number in case of emergency. He held the house extension up to the cell phone so that Sam could overhear what he could.

"We're at a hotel," Layla said.

"Where is the hotel? Do you know the name of the town? Or even the name of the hotel?"

"There was a sign. I can see it from our room. I can read, Daddy."

"I know, kiddo. Read me what it says."

"Sart...um. Sara... Sara-tug-uh. Sara-tug-uh Spa-rings Mo-tor Inn."

"Saratoga?"

"Yeah, I think so. Mommy said we could see horses here!"

"That's great. You're doing really well at reading."

She made a pleased little squeal. Then Jase heard Karen's raspier voice in the background. Then the line went dead.

"Did you hear that?" Jase asked Sam.

"Yeah. Waiting for the trace, but my partner is already on the phone with Saratoga PD."

"Karen's probably leaving the room right now."

"Yeah, but six-year-olds don't move real fast. If we play this right, we'll get a cop to the motel before she's able to leave."

"Should I go there? Should I go to Saratoga Springs to pick her up? If you arrest Karen, how are you going to get Layla back here? I don't want her riding with a stranger."

"How long is that drive? Two and a half, three hours, yeah? It's better to stay where you are. If she's on the move again, it's hard to say which way she'll go."

"I'm going." Jase got up and pocketed his cell phone. "Even if she moves this time, she can't get that far before we catch up with her again. It's better if I'm in the area, right?"

"Unless Layla is wrong."

"How can she be? What are the odds she'd misread Saratoga?"

"She's six years old."

"I'm going," Jase said, bounding out of the house.

"Yeah. Shit," Sam said. "Wait for me. I'll come get you."

Chapter Seventeen

Jase was worried that riding with Sam would be awkward, since he barely knew the man, but he found that, after they'd been on the road for about forty-five minutes, Sam's presence was calming. For one thing, Sam got regular updates from both the Saratoga PD and his own precinct, and he promptly relayed all updates to Jase. Beyond that, Sam was unfailingly steady, sympathetic to Jase, but otherwise tranquil.

Karen had, indeed, cleared out of the Saratoga Springs Motor Inn before the cops got there. She had paid cash for the room, but it was from a cash advance on her father's card, procured from an ATM in a mall three miles from the motel. "Not a criminal mastermind, your ex-wife," Sam had said when they found out about this piece of information.

And the thing was, Jase wanted to condemn her too. He was terrified and furious. But he knew also that she had parental instincts, the same way he did, and they'd told her that Layla was in danger. Her attempt to keep Layla safe was ignorant and misguided, but it was an attempt born of her need to take care of her daughter. And as mad as he was at Lowell and Karen for creating this situation, he was still angriest at himself.

"I don't mean to pry," Sam said, keeping his eyes on the road. "But I'm guessing there's more to this than your ex-wife kidnapping your daughter spontaneously. Usually there's a catalyst. Maybe it's not obvious, or one we can't explain, but I'm guessing you have some idea."

Jase wasn't completely sure he could trust Sam, but he wanted to. He said, "Yeah."

Sam glanced at him. "You don't have to tell me, unless you think it will help us find your daughter."

"I don't see how it's relevant."

Sam nodded. "Saw a case like this a few years ago. Mom took off with the kid because she didn't like Dad's new girlfriend."

Jase couldn't stop the sound that came out of his throat, a strangled moan, more of a gulp. The attempt to keep it down brought on a coughing fit. He realized when he calmed down that he'd given himself away. He sighed. "I had an affair."

"Ah. I had guessed. I don't need the details."

It spilled out anyway. "With my neighbor," Jase said.

Sam didn't even flinch. "Old Man Fisher's kid, right? Lowell?"

Jase thought of what Lowell had said the previous afternoon. If Jase needed someone to be there for him, to hold his hand, Lowell was it, Lowell was his man. Of course, that was before Jase had fucked everything up further by having sex with Lowell.

He said, "Yeah, Lowell. We broke up two days ago."

"Before or after Karen took off?"

"Before. And after. I don't even really know."

"That's a shit day," Sam said.

Jase coughed again, this time trying to suppress the bitter laughter. "Karen found out about my relationship with Lowell, and she's... I don't even know. Homophobic? Jealous? Crazy? So she took Layla. Lowell and I hadn't been seeing each other that long, but..."

"It's okay to talk about," Sam said. "For what it's worth, your secret's safe with me. And, believe me, I know all about secret affairs. I've been dating a firefighter from New Milford for the last eight months." He shook his head. "I thought cops were a bigoted lot, but, I mean, most of my precinct knows about me. I get some flak for it, but whatever. I earned my detective badge. No one can take that from me. A firehouse, though, Jesus Christ. I've never met a group of guys who spend more time talking about how to be a man. And, to these guys, being a man does not involve fucking other men. To put it crudely."

"I... Wow."

"Thought you should know. Does it help you trust me to know I'm gay? Or do you want to get out of the car now?"

"A little of both," Jase said.

Sam shrugged. "So, if you and Lowell were breaking up, and your relationship was the reason your ex-wife took Layla, why did she take off?"

"She didn't know we'd broken up. I guess I didn't realize..." What didn't he realize? *It's over? I want him back? I love him?*

It was that last thought that shut Jase up. He sank into his seat and looked out the window.

Sam's cell phone rang, meaning that Jase didn't have to talk anymore.

"Brown," Sam said into the phone. He listened for a long moment. "Yeah, I'm about twenty minutes from there, I think, give or take. Keep me updated."

"What?" Jase asked when Sam got off the phone.

"Saratoga PD found Karen's car in a parking lot. They haven't found Karen or Layla yet, but they can't be far. We're close, Jason."

"If they're not in the car, where could they be?" Jase's anxiety ratcheted up a few notches. Were they going somewhere on foot? Were they safe? Was Layla alone?

"Half the Saratoga police force is looking. We'll find them."

"We're twenty minutes away, did you say?"

"Give or take."

"Get us there faster."

Sam reached under the seat and pulled out a flasher. He rolled down his window and stuck the light on the roof. Then he stepped on the accelerator.

* * *

Lowell and Joanie sat curled together on the couch, watching an old horror movie to which Lowell was only half paying attention. He'd heard car doors slamming a few hours earlier. Since Joanie was there, and he didn't want to seem like a complete crazy person, he hadn't gone to see which neighbor's car had disappeared, but he felt pretty sure it was

Jase's. That meant there'd been some development in the case. Jase should have called. Why hadn't he called?

Of course, Lowell knew exactly why Jase hadn't called, but that hadn't stopped him from hoping he would.

Joanie squealed, then started laughing. "Goddamn, that's my favorite part of this movie. Gets me every time." She sat up and looked at Lowell. "Are you even watching?"

"I... No, I guess not." He rubbed his eyes. "I can't stop thinking about Layla and Jase. I'm trying to watch the movie but... I'm sorry."

"Hey, don't worry about it." She smiled. "You're worried about them. That's only natural."

"But do I even have a place worrying about them anymore? I mean, it seems pretty clear to me that it's over."

"Come on, Lowell. You don't really believe that, do you?"

He sighed. Part of him wanted to take back everything he'd said, to go back in swinging. Part of him thought he could still fix this, figuring Jase was upset because Layla was missing. Still, he knew that this argument had been brewing since before Karen had taken Layla, and if Jase wasn't willing to make a real relationship work, it probably wasn't worth fighting for. Knowing that didn't take away any of the sting.

"Maybe I should take it for what it was. Jase said he was just looking to get laid. So it was, what, a month of good sex. And that's all."

"That's so clearly not all."

"I feel like a complete dick for making this about me when Layla could be in trouble, and I know that's foremost on Jase's mind, but then I think I'll always lose to her, and then I feel like a terrible person and…"

"You're totally gone over him," Joanie said.

"I am." No sense in denying it.

"Don't push it now. I know you're hurting, and I also know you're scared shitless for that little girl. So wait and see what happens. Talk to Jase after this is over. Maybe there's still something to be salvaged."

"He was really mad."

"His daughter was taken from him."

"I was really mad too." Lowell sighed. "Can we just watch the movie?"

"Yeah. Let me make another bowl of popcorn."

* * *

Sam and Jase pulled into the parking lot ten minutes later. It was full of flashing lights and men in uniform, most of them surrounding Karen's silver Corolla. A small part of Jase hoped they had the wrong car, that Karen and Layla were still safe together in Karen's car, but when he and Sam approached, he recognized the license plate.

Sam introduced himself and showed his badge, then introduced Jase.

"Still no sign, sir," said a man in a brown suit. He pulled a badge from his pocket and showed it to Sam, then Jase. It identified him as Agent Garullo.

"FBI?" Jase asked.

"She crossed state lines," Garullo said. "That's when we get involved."

Jase supposed he should have been comforted by the fact that the FBI had gotten involved, but it made him feel more nervous.

"We got canvassers out?" Sam asked.

"Yep. We don't think she's here anymore, though."

Jase looked up and realized they were in a parking lot for a train station. "She got on a train."

Garullo nodded. "That's a very likely possibility. This station is unmanned this time of night. Passengers can buy tickets at machines inside. She didn't use her credit card to buy a train ticket, but she could have paid cash."

"Shit," said Jase. "If she got a train, she could be anywhere. If she's not in her car, how do we trace her?"

"We've searched the train station," Garullo said. "We've also interviewed the cab company that operates out of that building over there. No one meeting Karen's description, and no one with a kid has gotten a cab from there, but we've got a couple of uniforms trying every cab company in town, just to rule out that possibility." He sighed. "But, yeah. A train went through here twenty minutes ago, just before we got here. We think she probably got on it."

"Where are they?" Jase asked. "Can you stop that train?"

"We can, but the next stop is at Glen Falls, which isn't that far away. If she got off there, we might be too late."

Jase pushed away from the crowd and started bellowing their names.

Sam walked up behind him and put a hand on his arm. "Try to keep as calm as you can. Let the men here do their work. We'll find them."

Jase snapped. "You've been saying that for almost twenty-four hours now, and we don't have them yet, and you have no goddamn idea where they are!"

Sam steered Jase back toward the car. He pushed Jase into the passenger seat. "Just sit for a minute. I know you're worried and frustrated, but we'll figure something out, okay? You losing your shit doesn't help us find them either." His voice was stern, but not angry.

Sam walked away and joined the crowd of uniforms. Jase sat in the car. Sam had left the keys in the ignition, so Jase was able to fiddle with the radio. He found a baseball game— Mets vs. St. Louis—and found that the monotone of the announcer, the roar of the crowd, and the radio fuzz distracted him enough to ease a little bit of his tension, but he was still sick with worry.

I wish Lowell were here.

Jase wasted a few minutes talking himself out of that, but then he leaned back in the seat and felt the truth of it. He wanted Lowell sitting next to him in the car, trying to talk him down, offering words to console him. He wanted to be close enough to Lowell to smell him, to take comfort in the familiar scent. He wanted to be wrapped up in those arms, to hear Lowell whispering in his ear, he wanted...

His cell phone was in one of the cup holders. He wasn't sure that he'd be able to find Lowell's number if the screen was broken, but he could probably figure it out. If he could just hear Lowell's voice, even if Lowell shouted at him, that would be good. That way he wouldn't feel like he'd lost his mind. He wouldn't have lost *everything.*

"Jason!"

Jase moved to get out of the car, but Sam gestured for him to get back in it. "We're driving to Glen Falls," he said as he got behind the wheel.

"They got off the train." Jase was dizzy with panic now.

"I don't know. They stopped the train when it got to the Glen Falls train station. There are officers on the scene searching it now. We also sent a team to search the station, and a couple of officers are posted here in case they didn't get on."

"Oh God," Jase whispered, trying to calm down.

He couldn't speak as he and Sam sped toward Glen Falls. Sam got regular updates, but it was mostly various policemen ruling out locations. Three train cars had been searched. They weren't in the station.

Sam said very quietly, "I take it all back. If you want to freak out, go right ahead."

Jase ran a hand through his hair. Then they were pulling into another parking lot. Sam slammed on the brakes, and the wheels squealed as they pulled in front of the train station. They got out of the car. Agent Garullo pulled in behind them. He exited his car and jogged toward the station entrance. He was met by another cop, who said something Jase couldn't hear.

Sam grabbed Jase's arm. "Stay put," he said. He walked away before Jase could ask what was happening. Sam, Garullo, and the officer had a sotto voce conversation a few yards away, then nodded and split up. When Jase looked back toward the station entrance, he saw Garullo disappear inside.

Sam walked over. "Come with me," he said.

"What? Why? What happened?"

"We think they're on the train after all." Sam went into the station. Jase followed close behind him. "The officers who searched it didn't find Karen and Layla, but the man who works in the café car said he saw a woman and a child that meet their description. It's still a possibility that they got out here before the cops stopped the train, but they'd have to have gotten a cab, so we're checking with all of the cab companies. Even if they got off here, they haven't had enough time to get very far."

Sam told Jase to wait on the platform. He walked forward to talk to one of the officers on the platform. The doors on the train remained closed. Jase looked at the windows of one of the cars and saw a few confused faces. He also saw a man get up and walk to the end of the car. It didn't seem like it would be that hard to switch cars, or to hide in a bathroom, for that matter.

The train doors opened.

A dozen or so passengers, none of whom looked like Karen or Layla, walked out onto the platform. Then an officer ran down the platform, shouting, "Close the doors!" which caught the attention of a number of other people on the train. Suddenly, the platform was flooded with confused passengers.

Sam tugged on Jase's arm and pulled him back through the station. "Wait by the car. We've got to clean up this mess. I'm gonna make sure whoever authorized those doors to open gets fired."

"But..." Jase wanted to suggest he get involved in searching the crowd.

"No. Car."

Jase nodded. He was a little tired of being told to keep out of the way. He wanted to shout at Sam: That was *his* daughter, lost in the crowd up on the platform, if she was even there. There was a line of cabs waiting at the curb, each one displaying the name of a different cab company. If Karen had gotten off here before the cops stopped the train, she could have caught any cab and gone anywhere. Jase felt helpless. He didn't know how he would keep it together if he had to wait for her to use her father's credit card again.

There was shouting up on the platform. Jase moved to go back into the station, but then realized that, if Layla was found, Sam would bring her back out to the car. He had to stay in one place, just in case, so they'd find him. He wanted to scream.

Sam appeared at the door of the train station again. His face was red, and he breathed heavily. He walked outside. Then he smiled.

"We got them," Sam said.

Jase's knees buckled. He swayed as relief washed over him. He remembered to breathe again.

"An officer will be bringing them out in a moment. We're trying to get the chaos on the platform settled first."

Together, they waited. Officers went in and out of the building, and each time the station door opened, Jase bit his lip, waiting for Karen and Layla to emerge. Then, finally, they came outside. They were flanked by two uniformed cops and Agent Garullo.

Layla spotted Jase. "Daddy!" She tore away from Karen.

Jase sank down and knelt on the blacktop. The impact when she finally collided with him almost knocked him over, but he was determined to hold her. He threw his arms around her and hugged her close. He blinked to keep the tears at bay. "Oh my God," he said. "Oh my baby girl. You're okay, right?"

"I'm okay," she said. Her little arms came around his neck. "I missed you, Daddy. But Mommy said we had to go on this trip. I didn't want to go. I wanted to go to T-ball camp."

Jase laughed at Layla's child logic, and he also laughed out of gratitude and relief. She was in his arms, and she was safe and unharmed. He leaned his head against hers. "I love you so much, Layla."

She giggled. "I love you too, Daddy." Then she squirmed out of his arms. "What's happening? We were on the train and the train stopped. Now you're here." She scrunched up her nose.

Jase had no idea how to explain it. His relief was so powerful that he could just barely make sentences. He opened his mouth a few times, unable to come up with anything adequate to say. Finally, he tried, "I'm going to take you home so that you can go to T-ball camp." That seemed to satisfy her, though she still looked confused.

He managed to get his feet under him and stood up. He looked over at Karen. One of the uniforms took her arm. Sam leaned close to Jase and said, "You should get in the car. Let Layla say good-bye, then go to the car. She shouldn't have to see her mother get arrested."

Jase opened his mouth to protest, but now that Layla was safe, his worry and anger were fading. He closed his mouth again and nodded.

"Say good-bye to your mom, kiddo. We're going to go home now."

Layla started to walk toward Karen, but she stopped. She seemed confused. Her brow furrowed. "Mommy?" she said.

"Yes, Layla," said Karen, a pained expression on her face.

"I'm going home with Daddy now," she said.

"I know."

"Okay. Can you come to my T-ball game on Friday?"

Tears stung his eyes. How could he ever explain this to her? There was no way Layla could even begin to understand what was happening. It was likely she wouldn't be able to see Karen for a long time.

When Karen started talking, offering hollow possibilities, Jase turned to Sam. "What if I don't press charges?"

Sam shook his head. "Doesn't work that way. There are federal laws about whether parents can kidnap their own children. Karen signed away her rights when she granted you custody, so in the eyes of the law, she's not her parent. I dug up the court paperwork earlier today to be sure. She has some kind of visitation, right?" Jase nodded. Sam continued, "But it's a personal arrangement, not one made in the court?"

Jase watched Layla talk to Karen. "Yeah. Karen vanished
for six months after the divorce was final. We didn't see her
at all. Our visitation arrangement is kind of made up as we
go, because she tends to do that, to disappear for months at a
time. Layla spends one weekend a month with Karen's
parents, but we made that agreement after the divorce was
final. Karen sees Layla when she's in town, but it's sporadic."

"Even if you didn't want to press charges, Karen crossed
state lines, so that's a federal offense. There's some ambiguity
in this case, so it may not even go to court, but for now she's
going to be arrested. Agent Garullo will take her into federal
custody."

Sam walked over to Garullo and pulled him aside. While
they spoke, Jase went to his daughter. Layla said good-bye to
Karen, and then Jase steered her toward the car. "Are you
sure you're okay?" he asked.

Layla yawned as she climbed into the backseat. "What's
happening?"

"Nothing. You're coming home with me. Detective Sam
over there is coming back with us, I think."

"Is he a nice man?"

"Yes. He's a police officer."

Layla buckled her seat belt. "Can we see Lowell when
we get home? I missed him too."

Could they? That ship seems to have sailed, Jase thought.
Lowell had walked out, though Jase could acknowledge he'd
pushed him out the door. Could they salvage something?
Could Jase? Then what? It wasn't like they could be a real

couple. Layla was back, but nothing had changed. Lowell had been right.

"We'll see," Jase said when Layla repeated the question.

They waited in the car while Sam finished things up. Jase tried to distract Layla so she wouldn't see what was happening outside the car. She fussed a little, whining about wanting to be home, but by the time Sam got to the car, Layla had fallen asleep. Sam fetched a blanket from the trunk and handed it to Jase. He climbed into the backseat and draped it over Layla. Then he kissed her forehead and got out of the car. He closed the door gently.

When he looked up, a cop was pushing Karen into the back of a squad car. Jase sighed and got back into the passenger seat.

Sam said, "They're taking her into custody in Saratoga. Probably she will be moved to Fairfield County, but that'll be tomorrow at the earliest."

Jase was suddenly exhausted. He buckled up and settled into the seat. He closed his eyes. He heard Sam start the car and get it moving, but then he was out.

Chapter Eighteen

Lowell lay in bed for a while after he woke up the next morning. He'd thought he'd heard a car pull into Jase's driveway during the wee hours of the morning, which maybe indicated that Jase had found Layla. He wanted to call now, wanted to know what had happened, but he wondered if it was even his place anymore, if he had any business trying to reach out to Jase anymore, if he had any business caring.

He stared at his phone for a while, then sighed and got out of bed. After he was dressed, he decided to work for a while, hoping that Jase would call as promised in the interim. A few hours went by, after which Lowell looked next door. Jase's car was in the driveway, but the house seemed quiet otherwise.

Eventually, he gave up, packed up his things, and headed to Schuster's. At least getting away from his neighbor's house would lessen his distractions.

It worked for about twenty minutes before his mind started to wander toward Layla, toward Jase, wondering if it really was over for good, wondering why that made his heart ache so much.

He slid his laptop back into his bag and walked up to the bar. He ordered a diet soda from the bartender, some kid whose name Lowell couldn't remember. Then he sat, not sure what to do now.

Neal came in a short time later. After he handled the shift change with the bartender, he looked at Lowell. "Are you drinking?"

"Soda," said Lowell. "You gotta know, I never drink when I'm feeling out of sorts, for obvious reasons. I was too distracted to work at home, so I came here, but…"

"I just came from Jase's."

"Yeah? Is Layla back? Is she all right?"

Neal gave Lowell a long look. "Yeah. Jase had to drive up north to Saratoga Springs or some such last night to get her. Karen's in custody now, and crazy man that he is, Jase is trying to spring her, but she crossed state lines so it's a federal case now, I guess. This is all secondhand. I'm hazy on the details. But yes, Layla's fine. Very confused about what happened but unharmed. She seems to have thought she and Karen were going on vacation, but she said something about how it wasn't a very fun vacation because they kept switching hotels." Neal chuckled. "It's probably for the best that she doesn't understand what happened."

"Yeah. I'm glad she's okay."

"Jase didn't call you?"

"He said he would but…" Lowell shook his head. "We had an awful fight a couple of days ago, I don't know. I think it's really over now."

"So much unnecessary drama. And for what? It's not right, what's happening here. Jase should be able to choose who to love."

Lowell frowned. "If only it were that easy."

* * *

Layla was clingy all afternoon, but Jase didn't really mind. His boss had been uncharacteristically understanding of the situation, so Jase was taking his third day off work in a row and intended to spend it with her. She followed him around the house, so he played with her dolls, and colored in her coloring books, and sat through two really terrible movies.

While they were coloring, Layla said, "Lowell is really good at coloring."

"Yeah?" Jase said, his chest tightening.

"He draws really good too."

"He's an artist," Jase said.

"I miss him. Can he come over?"

Jase had seen Lowell's car pull out of the driveway earlier that afternoon. "I don't think he's home right now, but if he is, he's probably working."

Though, God knew, Jase missed Lowell too. Which was ridiculous, he told himself, because it had been only a day since they'd seen each other. Granted, that was when Jase had blamed Lowell for Karen taking Layla. He had meant it at the time, and there'd been a logic to that. But while it was true that none of this would have happened if it hadn't been for Jase and Lowell getting caught together, Jase wondered if he hadn't just sped up the inevitable, if this all wouldn't have come to a head somewhere down the line when Jase met someone else. Because Lowell was right; getting his kicks on his rare spare Friday nights, then coming back to Greenbriar to lead an otherwise celibate life was no way to live.

But even if he could reconcile with the fact that he would have to take some risks to be with Lowell, even if he were willing to make a commitment—and these were things Jase still wasn't sure he wanted—would Lowell even take him back?

The doorbell rang. Jase dropped a kiss on the top of Layla's head, and then he went to answer the door. He was a little surprised to see Joanie Reickert.

She breezed past him into the house. "I've got a bone to pick with you, Jason Midland."

"Please, come in, Joanie," Jase said with some sarcasm as he closed the door. He noticed she was holding several grocery bags. "What's going on?"

She turned to look at Jase. "I heard what happened."

"Oh. Well. Everything is fine now." He gestured toward Layla.

Joanie smiled. She put her bags down in the middle of the living room and held out a hand to Layla. "Hi, sweetie. I'm Joanie."

"I'm Layla."

"I'm a good friend of Lowell's. He's told me a lot about you. All good things of course."

"Joanie, why are you here?" Jase asked, starting to lose his patience.

"Well," she said. "As it happens, I was up until four a.m., watching horror movies and talking with Lowell." Jase tried to keep his face neutral, but knew when she nodded that he'd given himself away. Joanie grinned. "I'm volunteering."

"To do what?"

* * *

Lowell was still unable to work in the early evening. He sat in front of the TV and tried to eat some leftover pasta, not really tasting anything. When his doorbell rang, he thought it might be Joanie with more pints of ice cream—and that was something he didn't need any more of—but then he opened the door to a ruffled Jase.

"Hi. Can I talk to you?"

Lowell wanted to throw his hands in the air, giving up on trying to make any sense of what was going on between him and his neighbor, but he nodded and opened the door wider to let Jase in. "I heard from Neal that Layla made it back safe and sound."

"Yeah, she's good. We caught up with Karen upstate. I wound up driving back with Layla really late last night. Or early this morning, depending on how you look at it." He rubbed his forehead. "Can we sit?" He glanced at his watch. "I have, like, an hour, and I really want to talk to you about something."

"Sure." Lowell thought he sounded a lot more chipper than he felt. He motioned toward the couch.

"Joanie, of all people, came by the house and volunteered to babysit. Can you believe that?"

Lowell sat next to Jase. "She's meddling."

"I know." Jase put a hand on the back of his head and rubbed the hair there until it stuck out a bit. "She argued with me some too, but she made a valid point. If you feel anywhere as miserable as I have for the last few days, it's probably better to talk this out now that the dust is settling, you know?"

"I don't see how I could... I mean, your daughter was *kidnapped*. I can't even imagine—"

"It's been a rough couple of days." Jase stared unfocused at something near Lowell's television. "That was maybe the worst thing I ever had to go through."

"I'm glad she's okay."

"Yeah, me too."

Lowell watched Jase, unable to read his emotions. "There's all this shit between us now. I don't know how..." He shook his head. "Well, what I mean is that we shouldn't lose sight of what's important."

"I agree." Jase looked like he wanted to say something more, but Lowell cut him off.

"I'd been thinking that maybe you'd still let her come visit me now and then. I mean, she's such a great kid, and I was kind of surprised by how much I enjoy spending time with her." He'd been nervous about saying it, wondering if it was too presumptuous, but once it was out there, he was glad he'd made the suggestion. He didn't want to lose track of Layla. It was strange, but Lowell had almost started to feel a little paternal toward her. He never would have thought that possible.

Jase looked astonished. "Really?"

"Yeah, of course. I got her a little present, actually."

"You did?"

"I was shopping a few days ago and I saw this thing, so I bought it. Is it okay if I give it to her? Her birthday's coming up, right?"

"It is, yes. Well, anyway." Jase slumped forward. "That seals the deal."

"What does?"

"That you would want to spend time with my daughter even if you and I are not together. That you care about her enough to do that."

Jase started to reach over toward Lowell but then retracted his hand. Lowell would have happily fallen into Jase's arms, but he stayed sitting up straight and waited for Jase to finish talking. Jase shot him a half smile, but looked nervous.

"I care about you too," Lowell said.

Jase looked down. "Yeah. That's kind of what I wanted to talk to you about." He sighed. "I said some things the other day, and I don't know if I can apologize for them, because I meant them at the time. They felt true at the time. If you can't forgive me, I understand that."

"You blamed me for what happened."

"Yes, I did. Maybe I still do, a little. If you hadn't moved in... But how could you have known? I chose to kiss you, that time Layla saw us. I was there too. And in the end, I know Karen was in the wrong. She acted rashly."

"Okay," Lowell said. He bit his lip. He wasn't sure how to respond. He wanted to forgive Jase everything, but he'd been hurt by what Jase had said. He could put it aside, chalk it up to Jase being agitated because of the situation, but something else Jase had said that really bothered Lowell. "Even so, that's not the real problem here. If you can't get over this fear you have, if you can't—" He sighed. "You said we'd never have a real relationship. And if that's the case, maybe it's better if we didn't see each other for a while. I don't think I can just go back to being your friend as if nothing happened between us. Even just sitting with you now is so hard." Lowell looked down at his feet, not willing to look at Jase.

For his part, Jase was quiet for what felt like a long time before he said, "I had many moments last night, when Sam Brown and I were driving up to Saratoga, when I wanted you with me instead of him."

"Jase…"

"I had a lot of time to think when we were driving. It helped to, I don't know, put some things in perspective. Maybe it helped me understand what I really want. I didn't decide anything, but I…" He reached over and put a hand on Lowell's knee before taking it away again. "I don't know how to make a relationship work, but I'm not ready to let you go yet."

Lowell steeled himself and looked up. He thought about the last time they'd been in bed together, how intense it had been, the way Jase broke down a little at the end. He wanted to reach for Jase now, to ease the sad hang of his shoulders, but he remained with his hands in his lap.

"Are you really done fighting for me?" Jase whispered.

"I shouldn't have just walked out of your house yesterday. It was selfish of me, given what you were going through at the time. But I was upset."

"I know." Jase sighed. "I want you to fight for me."

"Jase…"

"See, because I was thinking in the car last night, while Karen was getting arrested, then later in the drive back to Greenbriar, I was thinking that I had my daughter back, so I should feel whole again, but I didn't because something was still missing." He put his hand on Lowell's knee again but left it there this time. Lowell looked at him, and their eyes met. Jase said, "I know now that the something is you. I can't figure out how to make this work. I don't know how things are going to turn out, but I'm in love with you, and I don't think my life is complete without you."

Lowell stopped breathing. He closed his eyes, wondering if he'd imagined what Jase had just said. In all of his fantasies of a moment like this, he'd never pictured it so heartfelt, so earnest, so well put. In his head, they made their grand declaration and swept each other off their feet. It wasn't this quiet little confession. But now that it had happened, Lowell thought this was better. This was real.

"Lowell?"

Lowell opened his eyes. "Say that again."

"Which part?"

"The part where you're in love with me."

"God, Lowell." It was clear he was fighting a smile, but then it got the best of him, and his face was completely changed by it. It the sort of smile that seemed so rare, the sort that lit up his whole face. "I love you."

Lowell wanted to remain stoic, wanted to let Jase sweat it out a little, but he couldn't keep the smile from his own face. "I love you too. I don't know why I thought I could live without you." He surrendered then and leaned toward Jase. He touched the side of Jase's face, then closed the space between them and kissed him slowly. When Jase's arms came around him, he knew this was the right move. Everything about this felt right and familiar.

Jase pulled away slightly. "Being with me is not going to be easy, but I want to try." Jase interrupted himself to kiss Lowell fiercely. "You were right. It doesn't have to be a contest or a choice." He kissed Lowell again. "I want you and Layla both in my life."

"I'm glad you finally figured that out," Lowell said.

"I'm amazed you forgave me this easily."

"Who says I forgave you?" Lowell pulled away slightly.

Jase laughed. He moved his face close enough to Lowell's to kiss him again. "I've got you."

"Yeah, yeah. I'm a sucker. But what about the other things you said, before Karen took Layla? You didn't want to be in a relationship. You just wanted to get laid."

"I lied." Jase sighed. "Well, when I slept with you the first time, I wasn't looking for anything more than that. But what I was doing, that was no way to get through life. The truth is that there's a part of me that was afraid to fall in love, and I still don't know how to do this, how to be in a relationship with a man, with you, but—"

"I'm not asking you to start a Pride parade in Greenbriar. I just want to be with you."

Jase kissed him again. "I didn't know how miserable I was until you reminded me how to feel happy. I realized sometime last night that I can't go back to that, to the way things were before you came into my life again. I mean, there's still a lot wrong, the job and this mess with Karen, but I think I can get through it if you're there with me. And I want to be there for you when you have problems. So I'm willing to try."

Lowell ran his fingers through Jase's hair and kissed him, really kissed him, opened his mouth and slipped his tongue through Jase's parted lips. Jase pushed Lowell back on the couch, into the armrest, in response. Lowell pressed his growing erection against Jase's hip, which got a moan out of Jase. He started thinking of ways to get Jase upstairs and then thought maybe that he had a condom in his wallet and wouldn't have to go that far.

"So, our meddling friend," Lowell said. "How much time did she give you?"

"She gave me an hour. That was"—Jase looked at his watch—"twenty minutes ago." He bowed his head and licked Lowell's neck.

"Mmm. Plenty of time." Lowell pulled Jase's shirt off. "I'm sure there's more here to talk about. Except… I don't know about you, but I'm kind of done talking for now."

Jase thrust his hands under Lowell's shirt. "Me too. God I missed you." He sat up, straddling Lowell, so that he could pull the shirt off. He did, and then he ran his hands over Lowell's skin. "Has it really only been a couple of days?"

Lowell laughed. It felt so good to laugh. He put his hands on Jase's waist. "I may never get enough of you," he murmured, running his hands up Jase's sides, over his chest, his fingers grazing the hair that spread across Jase's pectoral muscles. He traced the line of hair, sliding his fingers along the place where it tapered to a line before disappearing into Jase's jeans. Lowell admired; he memorized. He leaned up to kiss that chest, and he tasted Jase's salty skin. It felt like things were falling into place as he pulled Jase back close to him.

They kissed, and Lowell's blood rushed through his body. He wanted to get his hands all over Jase. He reached between them and undid the top button on Jase's jeans. Jase jerked, which surprised him. He pulled his hands away and placed them on Jase's back, holding him close as they kissed again. Jase wrapped a hand around Lowell's wrist and pulled it down. Then Jase pressed something foil-wrapped into his hand.

"Um," Jase said. "Joanie sent me prepared."

Lowell put the condom on the arm of the couch. "God bless that girl. Remind me to send her flowers. Now, come here."

He touched Jase's stomach, then kissed Jase as his fingers moved lower, feeling Jase's hot skin. He undid the zipper on Jase's jeans, then slid his hands in to touch Jase's cock. He was happy to find it hard and heavy against his hands. Jase gasped and hissed as Lowell wrapped his hand around it. Jase's skin was smooth and hot.

Jase wriggled out of his pants, then knelt on the couch, his body beautiful as the waning sunlight coming through the living room window bounced off his skin. Lowell moved to pull him close again, his most urgent desire being just to have their bodies pressed together. But Jase evaded him, then ran his hands down Lowell's chest, pressing his palms into the skin, then wrapping his fingers around nipples. The gentle squeeze and tug sent pulses of pleasure through Lowell's body, straight to his cock, which was now hard enough to make his jeans feel tight.

"Want you," he mumbled, reaching for Jase.

Jase still kept a little distance and then bent down and kissed Lowell's chest. His mouth traveled around Lowell's skin until it found a nipple. He sucked gently, and his teeth skimmed over the nipple, making it harden. Then Jase's hands traveled to the fly of his jeans and tugged at the button, unzipped the fly. Lowell groaned as need started to overtake him. He thought he'd go crazy if Jase just hovered there, if he didn't *do* something, touch him, anything. He looked down. Jase glanced up at him with a smile on his face.

Jase hooked his hands into Lowell's jeans and pulled them down along with his briefs. When all clothes were dispensed with and lying on the floor, Jase kissed the inside of Lowell's thigh. He trailed kisses all along the skin there until his face pressed into the space where Lowell's leg met his hip. Lowell felt him inhale.

"Jase…" he said, not sure how much longer he could put up with the teasing.

Jase chuckled. Lowell could hardly believe that. He felt crazy enough to crawl out of his skin, and Jase was laughing! But then Jase was wrapping his hand around Lowell's cock— finally!—and just as Lowell started to feel the barest of his needs begin to be satisfied, Jase slid his cock into his mouth. Jase's mouth was hot, and his tongue danced against Lowell's skin. Everything in Lowell seemed to harden and tighten, and he wanted to push farther, to keep that heat flowing over his skin, to pump and jerk and explode.

He groaned and arched off the couch. He ran his fingers through Jase's hair. Lowell couldn't remember Jase ever being quite this proactive in their lovemaking, and he loved every moment of it. Jase's tongue traced patterns on the underside of his cock, pushing at all the right spots, making warmth and electricity pulse through his body.

"I'm close," he said, "but I want to be inside you."

Jase backed off Lowell's cock. He kissed Lowell's stomach before he moved to reach for something on the floor. "There's lube in my pants," he said.

"You *are* prepared."

Jase handed the little bottle to Lowell. He straddled Lowell's chest, bracing his hands on the couch's armrest. "Get me ready," he said.

Lowell put his hands on Jase's head and pulled him closer. "Kiss me first."

"I love you," Jase whispered just before their lips crashed together. It took some maneuvering, but Lowell managed to get a fair amount of lube on his fingers before reaching behind Jase and finding his opening. Jase was breathing heavily, as if the anticipation of this was driving him as crazy as it was Lowell. They kept kissing as Lowell slowly pressed in one finger. Jase took a deep breath and relaxed against Lowell. He pressed in a second finger.

"I love you," Lowell said against Jase's mouth. Jase had to push away to allow Lowell's fingers to slide in and out of his body at a better angle. He put his hands back on the armrest and arched his back away, gasping and crying out as Lowell found his prostate. Lowell put a hand on Jase's back to steady him, and then he started kissing his chest as he stretched Jase, opening him up.

"I need you," Jase said, grabbing the condom from the armrest and pushing it into Lowell's hand. Lowell could not have explained later how he made it happen—if it was magic born of desperate, raw need, or what—but he managed to tear the wrapper off the condom, then roll it on himself. A quick thought about his poor couch and the possible destructive qualities of lube on black leather passed through his brain, but he dismissed it as foolish and figured that the man in his arms was far more important than his couch anyway. His body seemed to be yearning toward Jase as it was, his cock aching, his need to be inside Jase acute. He upended the bottle of lube and poured a healthy amount on his cock. He stroked himself to coat it.

Lowell gently pushed Jase back. Jase reached behind him and took Lowell's cock in his hand, and then, very slowly, he lowered himself onto it. Lowell watched his face, the brief moment where it was uncomfortable, then the easing in his expression when he relaxed his body enough to accommodate Lowell. Then Lowell was fully inside. He pulled him close. They sat like that, locked together on the couch, for a long moment before Lowell couldn't take it anymore and bucked his hips.

Jase rode him slowly. Lowell moved against him, the friction delicious as they moved with and against each other. Jase was tight and warm, and his body squeezed Lowell in all the right places. As he slid in and out of Jase's body, trying to draw it out and make it last, Jase kissed him hard, then trailed kisses over his face, repeating over and over that he loved him.

Lowell reached between them and stroked Jase's cock. Jase's eyes shut abruptly, and he moaned, clearly overwhelmed, and then he was coming. He threw his head back and was so beautiful as he came, his eyes slitted, his lips red, his skin glowing. His body constricted around Lowell as he shot in ribbons all over Lowell's chest. Lowell held him and continued to move his hips as he pressed his body into, against Jase. He closed his eyes as Jase's quivering body squeezed his cock. He was surrounded by the smell of Jase, of Jase's gasps and moans. His orgasm built slowly, rolling through his body like a stone picking up momentum as it tumbled down a hill, until at last he fell over the edge, pumping into Jase a few more times as he came, everything overwhelming. He kissed Jase desperately, needing to taste him, needing to be close to him. "I love you so much," he said when he was able to speak again.

Jase collapsed on top of him and slid his arms around Lowell's chest. He rested his head on Lowell's shoulder.

Lowell thought he should say something but could think of nothing that wouldn't sound trite or ridiculous. He kissed the top of Jase's head, figuring he could murmur some insufficient love words, something, but Jase's cell phone rang.

Jase sighed. He eased himself away from Lowell before grabbing his pants off the floor and extracting his phone from his pocket. He looked at the screen with some dismay. "The display is still broken. This might be important. Hang on." He straddled Lowell, then answered the phone, then waited while someone on the other end said something. He said, "Sure, fine, see you in a few minutes." He hung up and looked at Lowell. "Joanie and Layla are trying to make dinner and seem to be halfway toward destroying my kitchen." He climbed off Lowell and stood up.

Lowell sat up. "Okay." It figured, he thought, that just when he'd had this big moment with Jase, Jase would have to leave. He wondered if this was going to be what it was like to be in a relationship with Jase, if it would be a lot of sneaking moments and interrupted make-out sessions, of postcoital cuddling cut short. This, he supposed, was what dating a man with a child would be like. Stolen moments and T-ball games. So, maybe their relationship wouldn't be easy. Lowell decided it was worth the extra effort.

Jase started to get dressed, then looked at Lowell. "Come with me."

"Are you sure?"

Jase picked up his shirt. "Yes. Layla has been asking about you all day." He held out a hand to help Lowell stand.

He pulled Lowell up, and Lowell immediately put his arms around him. It felt so good to have his arms around Jase, to feel Jase's body pressed against his, to smell Jase's shampoo and aftershave and whatever else it was on him that smelled so good.

Jase kissed him again, then said, "Come on, get dressed."

They both cleaned up a little, then finished putting their clothes back on. Lowell grabbed the gift bag he'd put Layla's present in, then shoved his keys in his pocket and followed Jase next door.

Layla came running through the house when the door opened. She shouted, "Lowell!" before launching herself at him, so he caught her and picked her up.

"Hey, Layla," he said.

She hugged him tightly.

Joanie came out of the kitchen. "And all is right with the world again, I take it?"

"I don't know about that," Lowell said. He looked at Jase, who had a weird half smile on his face. "Things are good with us now, though, right?"

"Yeah," Jase said.

Joanie grinned. "I'm glad. I'm just going to finish dinner. Lemon Chicken à la Joanie, a specialty recipe of mine. It's just about ready." She turned on her heel and went back into the kitchen.

Lowell turned his attention back toward Layla, who still had her hands clasped behind his neck. "I have a little present for you."

"Really?"

That caught Jase's attention. Lowell felt him looking at them. He handed the gift bag to Layla. From it, she pulled the plush purple stegosaurus he'd found and a copy of the bunny book for which he'd designed the website.

"Wow, cool!" she said. "Thank you, Lowell!"

"You can show the book to your friends and tell them that you picked out the colors for the website."

Lowell stood. Jase looked at him, and everything was there on his face, pain and pleasure and longing and love. It was a pretty potent combination.

"Lowell, can you watch a princess movie with me?" Layla asked.

"How about after dinner, sweetie?" Lowell said. "I'll go see if Joanie needs anything."

"Okay." Layla smiled and crawled onto the couch. She opened the bunny book and started reading it out loud.

Jase followed Lowell into the kitchen. When she saw them, Joanie said, "Ah, menfolk. Jase, I don't know where you keep your plates and things. You guys can be in charge of setting the table while I put the food out." She picked up a casserole dish and carried it into the dining room.

As Jase pulled plates out of the cabinet, he said, "I wish you could stay the night. After what just happened, I don't want to sleep alone."

"Yeah."

"But I think it's still too soon. I don't want to freak out Layla too much."

"I understand." Lowell did understand, though he regretted that they would not have many nights together. He imagined that would change with time, though.

Jase smiled. He put the dishes on the counter. He walked over to Lowell and put his hands on Lowell's waist.

"I've never dated anyone with a kid before," Lowell said. "There's a lot of stuff I hadn't considered. How is she going to react to us as a couple?"

"I don't know. We can figure it out as we go."

"One thing at a time, eh?" Lowell smoothed the hair away from Jase's forehead.

Jase kissed Lowell then, and Lowell could tell it was supposed to be a quick kiss, but then Jase got stuck and instead started to explore Lowell's mouth with his tongue. Lowell responded eagerly, loving the way Jase kissed him, so sweet and tender and no longer hesitant. To think that this was a man who'd never kissed another man before Lowell.

"Ew!" said a voice from the doorway.

Lowell jerked away, but Jase held on to one of his belt loops, so he couldn't get too far. "Adults do such gross things," Jase said.

"I know!" said Layla.

"Is it a problem if I kiss your father?" Lowell asked.

"It's okay," she said.

"Okay. Good. Because I don't want to make you uncomfortable. If I ever do something you don't like, I want you to tell me, okay?"

"Yeah. So can we watch *Cinderella*?"

"After dinner, Layla," Jase said.

"That has the mice, right?" said Lowell. "Who make the dress?"

"Yes," said Layla.

Joanie came back into the kitchen then. She glanced at Lowell's hip, where Jase's hand still rested. "I don't recall setting a table involving much making out."

Jase smirked.

Lowell said, "Guess it depends on what you mean by 'setting the table.'"

"Dishes, boys," Joanie said. "Food's ready."

"Yay!" Layla cheered. She ran into the dining room.

"Well, there's an answer, I guess," Jase said.

Lowell smiled. "It's best not to keep a lady waiting."

Chapter Nineteen

Lowell waited with his mother in the exam room at the doctor's office. He had a feeling that the news was bad. His suspicion was bolstered by the fact that she was having a rough day. When he'd picked her up, she'd been confused about what they were doing that day. In the exam room, she kept quiet, and her gaze was absent.

He'd wanted to share his good news, that he and Jase were back together, and the future seemed so promising, but she kept staring at nothing and was barely responsive when he talked to her.

The doctor walked in. His mouth was set in a thin line. "Hello, Mrs. Fisher," he said. He walked over to her and gave her a cursory examination.

"It's bad news," said Lowell.

"Well," said the doctor. "There's no way to diagnose Alzheimer's with absolute certainty. Some causes of dementia are reversible and treatable. But I will tell you that I believe her memory loss will get worse with time. The tests we ran ruled out several other possible culprits. There are medications we can try. You might want to look into a home aide or make arrangements with the visiting nurse service."

Lowell felt a wave of guilt, wondering if he should have moved in with his mother, if he'd need to be around more often. The prospect of having to spend more time in that house filled him with dread, though. His stomach turned as he considered his options. None of them were good. "How long do you think she will be okay to live at home?"

"It's hard to say."

Lowell looked at his mother, who grunted. He wasn't sure if she was present enough to understand what was happening. She blinked rapidly and looked around the room. When her gaze settled on Lowell, he was unnerved. She looked at her hands where they rested in her lap. Lowell felt a wave of guilt; he should have come home sooner, he should have spent more time with her, and he should have known that it was getting this bad.

The doctor continued, "As long as she's still able to take care of herself, she should be fine to stay at home. As soon as she becomes harmful to herself, though, you will need to consider around-the-clock care."

Lowell's nausea intensified. He didn't want the burden of making this decision.

The doctor scribbled something on a prescription pad and handed the slip to Lowell. "We'll start her on this drug, which will delay the onset of symptoms and may help her memory improve. But you'll need to keep an eye on her, and I want you to bring her in for regular follow-up appointments."

Lowell took a deep breath. "All right." He took his mother's hand, but she barely reacted. He thought he saw her wince, but he couldn't be sure. "I'm not sure I can do this."

The doctor patted Lowell on the back. "I know this is difficult, but I think you'll do just fine. You did the right thing, coming to see me. We'll try the medication first, and if that doesn't help, we'll try other options, okay? I'll work with you to figure out what the best means of care are."

Lowell wanted his mother back. She still stared straight ahead, her expression blank. "Mom?" When she didn't respond, his eyes began to sting.

"I know you care about her. You can do this, though. You have my number, right? Call me if the symptoms worsen."

"Yes. I will. Thank you, doctor."

He drove his mother home. He made sandwiches for lunch and sat with her while she ate. She started to come back to herself later in the afternoon as they watched television. She laughed at something that happened on the screen.

"Mom?"

"I'm very tired."

He helped her lie down and stayed at the house while she napped, putting misplaced objects back where they belonged and dodging memories of his father. After a few hours, she woke up and was alert enough to ask about her doctor's appointment. Lowell explained the diagnosis, or lack thereof, and she took the news stoically. Then she said, "You will take care of me, right?"

"Of course I will," said Lowell. He hugged her. "Of course."

* * *

Jase woke up in the middle of the night and was pleasantly surprised to find Lowell in bed next to him. Lowell was asleep on his back with his mouth agape and looked a little silly but also untroubled, which was a good look for him. Jase smiled to himself and got out of bed. When he came back from the bathroom, Lowell's eyes were open.

"Sorry to wake you," Jase said.

Lowell yawned. "You got out of bed."

"Just to pee. I came back." Jase climbed under the covers. "Besides, this is my bed."

"And a very nice one it is," Lowell said, rolling onto his side. "I think we've sufficiently tested its durability tonight. The decor in this room leaves a little something to be desired, though. It's very…shabby chic."

"I don't know what that means," said Jase, settling against the pillows.

It had been sort of an experiment, inviting Lowell over. Jase wasn't quite ready to invite him for overnights when Layla was home, but on this particular night, she was sleeping over at a friend's. He'd never had a man in his own bed before, but he wanted Lowell there. He hoped these were the first of many nights together, but that was something he still had to work out, something he was still negotiating in his own mind. Still, in this moment, it felt nice to be there beside Lowell.

Lowell rolled over and snuggled up next to Jase. He said, "How much of this stuff did you replace when your parents...?"

"Not that much," Jase said. "The bed, that's really it. Karen wound up with most of our furniture in the divorce. It's all in storage, of course." He put an arm around Lowell. "I hope you're not critiquing my decorating skills. Your house is still mostly empty."

Lowell laughed. "I prefer to think of it as minimalist. Sure, there's not a lot of furniture, but what is there is very tasteful. No?"

"If you say so. Wouldn't hurt you to add some color. Everything in your house is black and white."

"Look, if I have to live in the suburbs, I at least get to decorate my house how I want. I always had this vision of living in a huge loft apartment with big windows, and I'd have my black leather sofa in the middle of this wide room with wood floors. The loft seems to not be a part of my fate, so I'm recreating it in my own little bit of vinyl-sided property."

"I know you're still adjusting, but I, for one, am glad you moved to the suburbs."

Lowell looked away.

"Aren't you?" Jase said.

"Yes. I was just thinking about my mother."

Jase ran a hand down Lowell's back. "Did you get in touch with that visiting nurse?"

"Talked to her this afternoon." Lowell pressed his nose into Jase's neck. "She's going to be able to stop by Mom's house a couple of times a week."

"That's good."

"For now, yeah."

Jase thought back on his own mother's illness. He never would have made it through her death if he hadn't had someone to lean on. "If you ever need anything, you want to talk or you need me to run to the pharmacy or if you just need a hug, I'm here, okay?"

Lowell lifted his head and looked down at Jase. His eyes looked a little watery, but he wasn't crying, exactly. "Thank you," he whispered.

"Of course."

Lowell rested his head on Jase's chest. "Yeah. So this is going to be interesting, eh?"

Jase smiled. "Yeah, looks that way." He knew he'd have to find a way to navigate a relationship with Lowell when Layla was home. He couldn't limit his time spent with Lowell to nights when Layla was away, especially now that Jase and Karen's parents were on the outs and Layla was spending less time with them. Lowell, for his part, wasn't pressuring Jase to do anything, for which he was grateful. He had time, he figured. They'd find a way to make this work. "In my experience," he said, "the best things in life are those you have to really work for."

Lowell ran a hand through Jase's hair before kissing him. "That's a sentiment I like."

"I love you, Lowell."

Lowell closed his eyes, then opened them again and looked at Jase. "Yeah," he said. "I love you too. We'll figure this out. For now, though, I'm happy enough just to be with you, to have this night together."

"Me too."

"So we do this one step at a time, yeah?"

Jase settled back into Lowell's arms. It was going to be hard, the road ahead. Kidnapping charges were still being brought against Karen. He struggled daily with figuring out how to tell Layla she couldn't see her mother for a while. He'd spoken with the authorities a few times, pleading for a lesser charge. It was unclear what would happen. In the meantime, he had to plan Layla's birthday party and get her ready for the new school year. He had a tough project starting up at work. Life would continue to move forward. But it seemed manageable if Lowell was at his side.

"Yes. One step at a time."

THE END

Kate McMurray

Kate has been writing since she could hold a pen. She's a nonfiction editor by day. Among other things, Kate is crafty (mostly knitting and sewing, but she also wields power tools), she plays the violin, and she dabbles in various other pursuits. She lives in Brooklyn, NY.

Loose Id® Titles by Kate McMurray

Available in e-book at www.loose-id.com and other e-book retailers

Across the East River Bridge
In Hot Pursuit
The Boy Next Door

In Hot Pursuit and *The Boy Next Door* are available
in print from your favorite bookseller

CPSIA information can be obtained at www.ICGtesting.com
Printed in the USA
LVOW050629200712

290710LV00001B/145/P